Where Kindness Lives
A Women's Fiction Anthology

Janet Koops | Annie M. Ballard |
Kimberly Nixon | Heidi McIntyre |
Sarah Branson | Cathelina Duvert |
Christy Matheson | Amanda Speights |
Paulette Stout

First edition. November, 2025.

WHERE KINDNESS LIVES: A WOMEN'S FICTION ANTHOLOGY

"A Place Where I Belong" copyright © 2025 by Annie M. Ballard

"The Bread Keeper" copyright © 2025 by High Plains Woman Press

"Cassoulet" copyright © 2025 by Sooner Started Press

"What She Would Have Wanted" copyright © 2025 by Cathelina Duvert

"The Backup Plan" copyright © by 2025 Heidi McIntyre

"World World" copyright © 2025 by Janet Koops

"The Irish Library in Kilkenny" copyright © 2025 by Christy Matheson

"The Birthday Wish" copyright © 2025 by Paulette Stout

"Mac and Cheese Love" copyright © 2025 by Roots and Wings Press, LLC

ISBN: eBook: 978-1-963745-13-9
ISBN: Paperback: 978-1-963745-14-6

Book cover design: Lynn Andreozzi

Published by Brown House Books, Colorado, USA

For information, contact: info@brownhousebooks.com or visit https://brownhousebooks.com

Contents

Introduction

In a world that often feels too loud, too fast, and too divided, kindness is a quiet force that can still cut through the noise.

The stories in this anthology were born from the belief that kindness matters. Kindness is strength, not weakness. And while it's not rare, it's often overlooked, so let us remind you of all the places where you can find kindness.

Each story you're about to read offers a different lens—a different heartbeat—on how compassion shows up in the everyday lives of women. Some stories are sweet. Some are complex. Some gently break your heart and stitch it back together again.

As you move through these pages, I hope you'll find yourself reflecting on the kindnesses you've received—and perhaps even feel inspired to pass some along. After all, kindness doesn't need an invitation. It just needs a place to live.

Welcome to *Where Kindness Lives*.

A Place Where I Belong

ANNIE M. BALLARD

The gulls were in fine form, filling the dim predawn morning with squawks and squabbles. I sucked in big gulps of crisp, salty air, and let the breeze lift my hair. Walking to work in June wasn't too bad. Even at four a.m.

I swung around the corner of the diner into the alley. Sonny's pickup sat under a streetlight that winked out as I walked under it, heading for the diner's back door. A skinny kid in a ballcap perched on the step, elbows on knees.

"Martin? What are you doing out here? Sonny's inside. You can go in."

He shrugged but didn't look at me. "It's locked."

"Don't take it personal. Old locks stick." I rummaged for my key, then shouldered the door open. "Sonny? You here?"

"Yeah." Muffled, but definite. Martin slouched in behind me, heading for the lockers. Sonny emerged from the walk-in refrigerator, arms full of cardboard egg trays. He was a big man, already wrapped in his white apron, tattoos bulging under his t-shirt sleeves, perpetual watch cap covering his bald head. "I'm here. Good morning."

"The door was locked."

"Sorry. It sticks." He put the eggs on the counter. "Good morning."

Rules of the Sunshine Diner per Sonny: Politeness is important. "Yeah, good morning. Martin was waiting outside."

"Yeah? Hey, kid, I'm sorry. Next time just bang on the door."

As if quiet Martin would ever bang on anything.

The morning routine was timed to the minute. I started the huge coffee urn before pushing through the swinging doors to the front of the house. There was plenty to do: fire up the espresso machine, brew more coffee, organize mugs, milk and sugar. Tune the radio to the maritime forecast. My hands were busy, but my mind wondered about Martin, Sonny's new stray. Martin had appeared last week, but he rarely came out of the dish room. He'd barely spoken a word. To me, anyway.

Sonny was clanging pots and talking, but not to me. I'd been collected by Sonny when I was a kid, ten years ago now. I wasn't exactly a stray, having a good mom and a home, and I sure talked a lot more than Martin (I recalled Sonny, exasperated, saying "Take a break, Motormouth.") but I had benefited from his kindness. Before the Sunshine, I'd been lost in an imaginary world of art, at least according to my mother. Working at the diner grounded me. Gave me another way to look at the world.

I was a stray who stuck. When I'd been running the front for a few years, I convinced Sonny to add a sophisticated espresso machine and send me for barista training. Together we turned the Sunshine Diner from just the fisherman's breakfast place to a tourist-forward coffee café. I made a logo, created social media campaigns, and soon our midday business was as brisk as early morning. I earned my place at the diner. I was the front of the house and Sonny was the back. He was the boss, of course. At least in his own mind.

Folks were waiting when I unlocked the front door. "Mornin', Cassandra." Ron Sheldrake elbowed past his brother. "Pour mine first."

"My idiot brother," Darryl muttered, following him. "Mornin', darlin." They headed to the counter, while others came in and took places at tables the booths on the far wall.

"Morning to you, too." I shifted into serving. Conversation grew as more folks came in, weather being top of mind. The chat got louder as I poured coffee after coffee, warmed doughnuts, and took orders. Sonny had plates up already, standing orders for our regulars.

I plunked pancakes and a hunter's breakfast in front of the Sheldrake brothers, and they made the usual big deal about me getting the order backward, but it was a joke, like always. The customers, mostly fishermen, came in waves, and I hustled: taking orders, delivering food, filling cups, and trading insults and jokes.

Twenty minutes later, Ron and Darryl parked their big thermoses on the counter and headed for the cash register, followed by others.

"Martin! Fill-up time."

Martin lugged the big coffee urn from the kitchen. The kid was skinny but strong, I'd give him that. Soon we were in a rhythm, Martin filling the fishermen's thermoses with coffee, me handing out to-go bags with doughnuts, molasses cookies, and Nanaimo bars, taking payments and making change. In the middle of all this, more folks came in, took seats, and greeted Sonny and me.

"Who's the new kid?"

"This is Martin. He's here for the summer."

By the dozenth repetition, Martin's face flushed pink, but he kept up with the coffee demand. He even replaced the big urn with a fresh one from the kitchen without being asked.

At eight, we had a breather. Two tables of families with kids had just been served and nobody new had arrived. Martin took a bin of dirty dishes to the back, and I followed with a second one. He rinsed and I racked the plates, mugs and silverware in silence, Sonny's kitchen music—classic rock—as a loud accompaniment. Sonny scraped the grill then headed out the back door.

"Where's he going?" Martin's voice wobbled.

"He's just having a smoke." The kid looked terrible: stark white face, shoulders slumped, trembling lips. Even his hands were shaking. "Hey, are you okay?"

"I don't know."

"Did you eat today? Come on."

Sonny arrived back in the kitchen when I was scrambling eggs in a stainless bowl. "Martin needs breakfast," I announced.

"Is that right? I'm the cook in this kitchen." He took the bowl from my hands. "You, Martin, you go have a seat." He nodded to a step stool beside the counter. "Stay in your lane, Cassandra."

I laughed and shot Martin a look, but he was too miserable to get in on the joke. "You want a muffin?" He shrugged, but I split one of our cranberry-walnut muffins and popped it onto the grill. "You gonna yell at me about that, too, Sonny?"

He elbowed me out of the way when the doorbell jangled out front. "Okay, I'm going. Thanks for this morning, Martin. You did great."

When the kid looked up, for the first time there was a bit of light in those dark eyes. As Sonny laid a plate of food in front of him, I heard my name being called from the front.

After closing that afternoon, Sonny came out to sit at the counter. I was still filling salt shakers.

"Martin perked right up after he ate. Boy's still growing, probably needs to be fed before work."

"And too young to know it, yet." I couldn't help my tone. Some of Sonny's rescues had been more work than help.

"He's a good kid. You two are gonna get on okay."

"He won't talk to me. It's like he's scared of me or something."

Sonny chortled. "I'm sure he is. You're a female. A girl person."

"To a kid his age, I'm not a girl. I'm twenty-five - as old as his teachers. I'm sure he doesn't think of me as a girl."

"Maybe you have a reputation as a tough nugget."

"Pffft." I flicked my towel in his direction. "Listen, I'm due at work. Can I go now?"

"You got that application done?"

I gritted my teeth but made my voice calm. "I'm still working on it. It's kind of a big deal, you know."

"Don't wait too long."

"Yeah, yeah," I muttered, heading for the door. "See you in the morning."

My daily walk to the gallery usually helped me settle from the rush of the diner. The gulls were still arguing, the salt air still crisp, but now I could snatch sunlit glimpses of the cove between buildings. Too soon, the gallery loomed on my left.

As I pulled the heavy oak door, the quiet rushed out to meet me. Before I had a chance to relax, Leonard jumped to his feet from where he'd perched on the edge of the desk. All polished shoes, impeccable attire, and crisp articulation, he was the gallery owner and my other boss. He could not be more different from Sonny. Leonard would never survive working in a diner.

"Thanks for showing up," he snapped. Hoisting his briefcase, he headed toward the door, but stopped when he got to me. "I'm late."

"I'm not late. You probably just overbooked yourself." Again.

He glanced at his watch and his face relaxed. "You're correct, of course. I'm sorry. I hate feeling rushed."

"I'm sorry you feel rushed." We could do this dance all day.

"My own fault, as you pointed out. Today, please work on that grant proposal, and call the list of potential sponsors for the October show. It should be a quiet afternoon."

"Yeah, that's fine." Quiet sounded great. I edged past him toward the desk, but he was immobilized, staring at me.

"Aren't you in a hurry?" I eyed him. "You're late, remember?"

"Did you finish your application?"

Bam. Right in the solar plexus. "We can talk about that later."

"University deadlines are real. There's no special treatment."

I thumped my backpack onto the desk. "I don't expect special anything, except for you and Sonny to lay off. I'll get it done."

"Sonny, too?" Leonard chuckled. "We'll 'lay off' as you say when you submit it." He turned toward the door, missing my eye roll. "Goodbye."

When the door creaked closed, I sank into the desk chair, surrounded by comfort and soporific ambient music. Despite the gallery's open sign, most business was transacted online by Leonard. I was a live body in the afternoons and did some admin stuff. Rarely, I got to help hang a show or research catalogue copy. Those were the best days, when I could see myself as a researcher and writer.

But today was not that. I popped in my ear buds and cranked up my favourite podcast (*True Crime and Art: Thefts and Forgeries*) while I worked. By six p.m. exactly nobody had been by, but my assigned tasks were done. As I loaded my backpack, the door groaned open. "Cassandra?"

"Evie! When did you get back?" Evie had worked at the gallery a couple of years ago.

Her smile was as wide as her arms as she reached up to hug me. "It is so good to see you," she said.

I hugged her hard. "You, too. What brings you here?"

"You! I haven't seen you in over a year." I had never understood our strange friendship; she was a real artist getting her PhD in art history, and here I was with my certificate in barista skills. Evie was ten years older than me, too, though that difference didn't seem as important as the ten years between Martin and me. "How are you doing?"

"Good enough. What's grad school like? And how's Stephen?" Evie met her partner, an American artist-scholar, when he was in Stella Mare on sabbatical. It was a whole romantic story.

Evie glowed. "I love it. I wasn't so sure, as you know, but I'm doing research on women's art-making history, and nobody thinks that's weird. I've found my people, you know? It's just what I needed. What I hoped for." When she looked right at me, I could see it coming. "How's your application?"

"You've been talking to Leonard."

"Well, Stephen has. You know we're all pulling for you, right?"

"Yeah, I know." How could I not, when every conversation included some reference to this process? So annoying. Well-meant, but irritating.

She laughed. "You're such a prickly pear. We just want to support you." She actually patted my shoulder. "Remember, I've been in your situation."

"You were never in my situation. You were an artist, not a waitress."

"A waitress? Is that what you call yourself?"

I leaned against the desk and folded my arms. "That application..." It was brutal to see myself from the outside in, and made me sick to my stomach, literally. Twenty-five years old and not one thing to show for it. I'd spent my first couple of years after high school making art between shifts at the Sunshine, but really, nobody cared. Not even me.

I loved art, but it didn't make me an artist. I loved other people's art, old, new, and everything in-between. When Leonard offered me a job, I thought I'd get closer to the art, but admin work wasn't doing it. It helped pay the bills, that's all.

Looking thoughtful, Evie said, "What if you think about your skills, not your job? I can help you."

My chin went out. "No sugarcoating. I'm a waitress. That's it."

"You're good at it, too. Does it ever get busy? Do customers like you? Did you turn the Sunshine into a tourist destination, not just a fisherman's breakfast joint?"

"Well..."

"You handle stressful, busy environments, create smooth interpersonal relationships, assess community needs, and create systems to address them."

I wanted to say no, but I couldn't, because it was true. "That's quite a spin."

Evie was brisk. "No spin. Facts. Talk about your skills. Are you free for dinner? I'm leaving in a couple of days, and I really want to hang out with you."

"Promise we won't focus on my application the whole time?"

"Promise! I have lots to tell you about my work. And my nasty supervisor. Come on!" She tugged on my arm. "If we go now, we might get a lobster roll at The Wharf before they run out."

Before opening time the next morning, Sonny called me into his alcove. "I want you to start Martin on the espresso machine."

"He's already doing pretty well with cleaning it."

"That's not what I mean. I want him to learn them fancy coffees."

"You mean my fancy coffees. Martin's the dishwasher."

"There's more to that boy than you see. Teach him."

"Sonny..."

He looked over his glasses at me. "Do it, Cass."

My sigh was probably audible out in the dining room. "I don't know when that's going to happen. We don't have much free time."

"Make some," Sonny said unhelpfully. "I want Martin up to speed on barista drinks. Right away. Got it?"

Shocking wetness stung my eyes. "I'm the barista, Sonny."

His look felt cold. "Teach the boy."

I glared toward the alcove that held the sinks and dishwasher as I returned to the front. Had Martin heard? Could he even take instruction? From me?

I kept my distance until after I locked the door at two. Grim, I marched into the noisy dish area. Martin was facing away, spraying down the sinks and counter while the big stainless commercial dishwasher roared.

I had to shout. "Martin! Come on!"

He emerged from the cocoon of noise, looking puzzled.

"Sonny wants you to learn to make espresso."

He lit up. "Okay. Now?"

"I've got a few minutes before my other job," I said tightly. "So yeah, now." Out of the corner of my eye, I caught Sonny smirking in my direction. "Let's go." I jerked my head toward the front.

Leonard paced the gallery that afternoon, snatching glances at me with a disturbing little smile. I stared at the laptop, but I could still see him. Heck, I could *feel* him looking at me.

"Stop it, Leonard."

"Whatever do you mean? I'm not doing anything."

"You're looking at me." I sounded like a kid fighting with her brother.

"So?" The smirk remained.

"Really, Leonard. I can't work this way. You're just so smug."

He leaned across the desk. "I heard the good news."

My shoulders sank. "What news?"

"Evie said you submitted your application." He chortled. "Finally! I guess the third time's the charm."

Shame burned my face. How did he know? "Yeah, she fed me a lobster roll, then made me finish and send it."

"Food first. I didn't know Evie was so strategic."

"Can you please keep this a secret? I can't believe she told you."

"Well, Stephen did, not Evie, but why secret? It's just an application."

"I don't want to have to tell people when I get rejected." I sank even lower in the chair.

"Pfft! You'll get in. I'm sure of it."

I knew then there would be no secret. Leonard loved sharing everyone else's news.

The whole thing—my imaginary path to becoming an art curator, university then grad school—it was so remote, you know?

It was a fantasy, not something real. It was my dream, a place I could go when things were not great in the real world.

The only problem was now I'd applied to school. I might have killed my dream trying to make it come true, and I couldn't even pretend I hadn't. Leonard would make sure everyone knew.

On day three of barista training, Martin showed up with a new recipe idea. By the end of his first week, he was pulling coffees, wearing the Barista-in-Training badge I made for him. People—especially teenage girls—liked his drinks. Or maybe his dark eyes. His head was up, shoulders back, and he even made eye contact.

Heck, he talked to me.

"Listen to this," he said, reading from his phone. "'A good barista can provide not only an espresso, but an experience. A good barista is informed and passionate about their occupation. A good barista is an ambassador, teaching people how to appreciate coffee, helping consumers identify tastes, and educating them on what to buy, what to drink, and what to trust.'" He looked up. "That's on the Canadian Barista Institute."

"You're doing homework." I might have underestimated this kid.

"I like doing the coffee. I even like the customers."

I had to smile. "You sound surprised."

"Yeah, a little. As a dishwasher, I wouldn't have to talk to anybody."

"You're doing great talking to customers, though."

Sonny came through and gave Martin a pat on the shoulder, then tossed me a wink before he headed back into the office alcove. Guess Sonny knew what his stray needed.

The fat envelope from Mount Allison University was addressed to me at the gallery. It shook in my hand. Whatever it said, I didn't want to know. I stuffed it, unopened, into the bottom of my backpack.

Of course, there was an email, too.

"We are delighted to inform you... bursary funds ..."

Shaking, sick to my stomach, the walls closed in. I snapped the laptop shut and headed to the back room of the gallery. Maybe tea would help.

I leaned against the brick wall while the kettle heated. The rough texture felt good. Reminded me to breathe. Shaking, I only spilled a little boiling water. I returned to the wall, inhaling peppermint steam while trying to compose myself, but neither tea nor deep breaths slowed my pounding heart. Maybe I should call an ambulance.

But no. This was panic, pure and simple. I could not succeed at school. It was too easy to imagine my failure. Twenty-five-year-old first-year student, dumb, incapable. Kicked out at midterms. Dragging the shame of failure all the way home. If I left home, failure was my destiny.

Sick already at the thought, going away was impossible. I couldn't feel like this and function. But nobody knew I'd been accepted. Nobody would ever know. I was good at keeping a secret. Nobody had to know. I could stay here, stay at the Sunshine and the gallery. Stay where I was capable and wanted. My chest eased.

I dug the fat envelope out of my backpack and lit a match to the corner. I watched it burn in the sink, then poured my tea on it and returned to work.

I was not a liar, but I could turn a conversation around. When people asked, I'd say, "Oh, well, I'll hear when I hear," and change the subject. Evie was back in the States, so it was safe to tell her the truth when she texted. I was needed in Stella Mare. Soon enough, everyone would forget I ever applied for school. I was home free.

The August holiday weekend was predictably frantic. Sonny found a new stray for the dish room—another kid, maybe seventeen but talkative—so Martin came up to help me run the front of the house. This was peak tourism. Extra hands were welcome.

Visitors thronged the gallery. Instead of second-guessing my life decisions, I helped guests find exactly the right boring lighthouse watercolour. I knew they wanted souvenirs rather than art, but I appreciated their desire for something to remind them of Stella Mare.

When I got to the gallery on Thursday, Leonard was closeted in the back room while a half dozen visitors gazed at art. I dumped my backpack, tidied my hair, and went to greet the visitors. While listening to a white-haired lady talk about grandchildren, Leonard came from the back, followed by Sonny. Impossible.

Something terrible must have happened. I excused myself to speed-walk over to my two bosses. "What's wrong?"

"Hi," Sonny said. "I came to see where you spend the other half of your life."

I scowled. "This is no social visit."

Leonard wore an outright grin. He clapped Sonny's bicep, the closest he could get to the big guy's shoulder. "I don't know what you mean. My friend Sonny can come by any time he wants."

They shook hands, all smiles, and Sonny left the gallery. Something was up and I was left out. "Really, what's going on here?"

"Really, nothing to concern you."

"Don't mock me, Leonard."

He nudged me. "Look, somebody wants to buy something." The white-haired lady stood beside the watercolour rack, tapping her toe. I hustled over.

We were busy all afternoon. After locking up, Leonard smirked at me, like he was in on a joke I didn't know. I hated that look. Suddenly, the smirk evaporated and my irritation bloomed into anxiety. Something was up.

"Sit down, please. After August 15th, I'm going to let you go."

"What?" The words hit like a sledge to my gut. I snuffled back the instant tears, of course. "We're so busy. What are you going to do? Without me?"

He looked away. "That's not your problem. Your job ends next week. If you decide to quit earlier, let me know."

Was it the way I left that New Jersey lady hanging? "What did I do? Why are you doing this?"

"I can't keep you on," he said more firmly than I'd ever heard Leonard speak. "Consider it a layoff. Now go on home."

He basically shoved me out the door. It made no sense. How could he fire me? This was MY job. My chance at something better than just being the waitress at my hometown diner.

I stumbled home, where I pounded out a long, impassioned email to convince Leonard of his mistake, but something, maybe pride, kept me from sending it. I wasn't going to beg. No way. He'd be sorry as soon as he had to work from open until close. Do his own social media. Write his own grant proposals. He'd be sorry.

Maybe I could add a day at the diner. The weekend staff might like some time off. Besides, it wasn't like Leonard was paying me much. I'd ask Sonny in the morning. Finally, I settled into sleep.

My four a.m. alarm woke me from a dream in which I was floating through golden light like some impressionist landscape, but when I lifted my head my golden dreams fled the scene, leaving my devastated heart.

Leonard was right to lay me off. I was an imposter. A loser. I didn't even need to go away to school to fail. I could fail right here at home.

The predawn gloom matched my mood. I dragged into the Sunshine an unprecedented ten minutes late. Sonny's rock 'n roll assailed my tender heart, but Martin and Sonny were hard at work. The kid was hauling dishes, Sonny banging pots, and I was glad to be in a familiar place, where people needed me. Wanted me. I almost forgot my gloom.

But when Sonny called for me to sit in the office alcove, that unholy vision of Sonny and Leonard shaking hands at the gallery loomed. It had been so weird, and then Leonard canned me. I didn't want to listen to Sonny.

"We've only got twenty minutes."

"Sit." He sat, too, heavily. His face was serious. "I have to tell you something."

When it came, it still hit like a hammer.

"I'm letting you go, Cassandra. The fifteenth is your last day."

It was worse than yesterday. Ten years of my life worse. If Leonard's rejection had been a bomb, this was nuclear. My world was exploding. "Are you guys colluding? I just don't get it."

He frowned. "There's nothing to get. As of August 15th, you're finished at the Sunshine Diner. It's been a good ten years, but you're done."

This time the tears didn't stay put. My face was wet; drips fell off my chin. I could not speak.

"Oh, Cassandra, don't do that." He rummaged for a paper napkin, shoving it in my hand.

"Why?" I wailed. Embarrassing, yes, but I didn't have much control. "Why are you and Leonard doing this to me? I'm a good employee."

His chin got very firm. "It's done, Cassandra. Now you better get going. Almost time to open."

"What's wrong with you? Do you think I can work like this?" I buried my face in my hands, sobbing, but not before I saw him signal to Martin, who headed out to the front of the house.

"Get it together. Do you want me to call your mother?"

A spike of rage instantly dried my tears. "Stop it, Sonny. I'm not one of your kids." I wiped my face, stood with exquisite dignity, and headed out front. I would face my customers, just like always, greet them, parry their insults, get them through their morning. Sonny wasn't going to take that away from me. Martin might make good coffee, but he wasn't me.

I snapped at Martin to get the creamers out, but he had done all the opening work. It wasn't his fault Sonny lost his mind, but maybe it was my fault. I'd done too good a job of training this new barista. What was Sonny going to do when Martin had to go back to school? What was Sonny going to do without me?

Somewhere inside a tiny voice asked, what are you going to do without this place, these people? But I couldn't think about that now. Now I had people to feed, coffee to pour.

When the shock left, I was furious at Leonard and Sonny. I hated Martin for being a quick learner. I was mad at myself for training my replacement. Leonard never really gave me a chance. All awful people, messing me up. Ruining my life.

Online job listings confirmed what I knew. There were no options in Stella Mare. I'd have to move, leave town as a failure. Jobless, future-less, I had to work through the fifteenth just for money, but after that? I didn't need to go to university to fail. I could do it right here at home. The worst thing I could imagine had already happened.

I knew they wanted me to go to school. But did they have to be so brutal? Leonard was sharp and edgy, but Sonny had been almost like a dad. My heart hurt so much.

Despite myself, I pulled up the email from Mount Allison University and read it for the first time.

Yes, they accepted me, and yes, they offered financial support.

They wanted me. Somebody wanted me, even if the message arrived in a form letter. There was a button to push if I wanted to accept their offer, and of course I had to send them a deposit. That gave me pause.

I sent a quick text to Evie in North Carolina. Then another to my mom, about the deposit. I hated asking for money, but Mom had always wanted me to go to uni. Their replies arrived instantly. I could almost feel these two women supporting me as I straightened my back and clicked the Accept button on the university email. Then hastily, I thumbed a reminder to Evie and my mom to keep this absolutely quiet.

My last day at the diner was kind of regular. Nobody knew I was leaving except me and Sonny, so things went on as usual. I might have cried a little when I locked the door and handed over the big skeleton key to Sonny. But I just stuffed everything in my backpack and took my last walk down Water Street to the gallery, stopping off at the wharf to listen to the gulls argue over pizza crust and the boats chug in and out of the harbour. I didn't much care if I was late.

When I finally pushed open the gallery door, it was oddly dim and quiet, not even any of Leonard's mood music. When the heavy oak door thumped closed, the place exploded with light and sound.

"Surprise!" Noisemakers, music blaring, and people shouting. "Good luck!"

A big cake adorned the desk, and a hand painted banner hung above it. The gallery was full of fishermen, cleaned up after work, and other local people. Leonard and Sonny were laughing together.

"You guys." I was a little choked up. "You suck, you know that?"

"Aww, we love you, kid." Sonny grabbed me in a one-armed hug. "You just needed a big push to do the right thing."

"Why does everybody think they know what's the right thing for me?" I looked around the gallery, catching eyes and waves and smile. "Even the Sheldrake brothers?" Darryl and Ron were arguing over something near a punchbowl.

"Nah. They just want to give you a good send-off."

I scoffed. "You and Leonard were pretty harsh. I don't think you had to actually fire me."

"Leonard didn't want to do it. I made him."

Leonard wore the smirk. "It worked, didn't it? Sometimes we're just too comfortable doing the same old thing." The smirk softened into a real smile. "I'm going to miss you but I think you'll love your next step."

Sonny leaned in. "Listen, kiddo, you can make a go of anything. I've seen it. Even baby birds have to be pushed from the nest. They probably think it's harsh, too."

"Sonny, how poetic!"

He looked abashed. "Yeah, so you just keep flapping them wings."

"I will keep that in mind. I don't think baby birds get a party, though."

Leonard tugged at my arm. "You have to cut the cake."

"Okay." I allowed him to propel me toward the big sheet cake with "Congratulations Cass" written in red icing. "Wow, Sonny! My favourite kind. You've been listening."

"Yeah. So cut your cake, but remember, this party is nothing compared to the one we're going throw when you graduate."

Graduate? Me? Well, it was possible. "I've been pretty busy hating you guys for a week, you know."

"Yeah, but you love us now." Leonard handed me a knife for the cake.

Sonny stood in front of me, hands on hips, watching me slice the cake just like he'd watched for the past ten years, every time I tried something new.

"What? Am I doing it wrong?"

"You're doing it your way. The way you do everything. Just right."

I had to look down at the cake to hide my tears. "Yeah, Sonny. I got this."

"I know that. Sounds like you know it, too." He nodded.

Handing Leonard the knife. I skirted the table to launch myself at Sonny for the biggest hug I had.

About Annie M. Ballard

Annie M. Ballard writes light, heartfelt women's fiction set against the backdrop of Canada's beautiful Maritimes. After a long career as a psychologist, she now brings her insight into relationships, family, and resilience to the page, crafting stories that celebrate women finding their way through life's challenges with courage, humor, and love.

Her characters feel like friends you'd happily share coffee and laughter with—whether it's four sisters learning to reconnect, a daughter searching for the father she's never known, or, in this anthology, a small-town barista discovering just how much her life can change (with a little "help" from those around her).

For more information about Annie and updates, go to: https://anniemballard.com/

The Bread Keeper

AMANDA SPEIGHTS

The mild tang of sourdough lingers in the air as I gather the bread. I have three round loaves left from what I didn't manage to sell or trade today. The cabin glows with warm light from the lamps and hearth, but the fire does little to ease the dread of stepping out into the cold night.

I hang my apron, wrap my shawl around my shoulders, and put the loaves in a basket.

"Come on, boy." I pat my leg, calling the dog. I still don't know where he came from, only that he's been a fine companion since the day I caught him eating a pan of biscuits he'd knocked onto the floor. Unfortunately, or fortunately based on how I look at the turn of events now, I'd left the cabin door open for just a moment while helping Jillian Bixby to her wagon. She'd traded me flour and butter for bread. Thankfully, the biscuits were meant for me and not a customer.

I'd shooed the dog out the door with my broom, but he refused to leave. He whined and ducked his head, remaining in the house. Looking as sad as I felt, peering at me through drooping eyes, as if asking for mercy.

Entering the woods, my thoughts go to the girl I often see at the clearing near the berry patch. I don't believe she's much younger than myself, but I do know her as being a daughter of Jed Hollis. I never approach. Just back away slowly, leaving her to the fruit I know she and her family need more than I—a young widow with no one to care for but myself.

It angers me what the town of Juniper is doing to this family. Yes, Jed Hollis fought for the rebs in the war. The same war my husband proudly fought for Mister Lincoln. Unfortunately, my James didn't return. I don't hold that against Jed though. Was he wrong? The town folk would say yes, but perhaps he was only doing what he had to, just as James and many others did. The people of this town are in no position to judge. We have all sinned, and no sin is greater than any other.

There have been rumors of thievery, and each time the town folk get themselves all fired up about it being Jed Hollis doing the stealing.

Mother moon, full and bright, lights my way through the forest. I waited specifically for this night, the harvest moon, the perfect night to leave the bread in the clearing for the Hollis girl to see and take home.

Her frail frame appears as if she gets very little food. They must rely solely on the land, which isn't easy in these mountains. They're called the Rockies for a reason. The town refuses the family all manner of services, and I know Jed and Temperance Hollis are too proud to accept what I may take to their door. I tried once. Told them it was a welcome gift. Missus Hollis nervously thanked me but stated they wouldn't be beholden to anyone with the way the town has treated them. They couldn't take any chances.

When I reach the space where the woods open, I notice a shadowy figure tying rabbits to a tree limb. A stick cracks under my foot, and the man turns to me.

It's Gideon Knox.

"Hattie Mae." He stands back as I approach.

The moonlight catches the scar that runs from the corner of his mouth to his cheekbone—the scar he brought home from the war. Gideon was one of the lucky ones who returned. Not the same, but alive nonetheless.

He stomps towards me with a slight limp.

"What are you doing out here? Are you mad, woman?" He glances at the dog beside me. "And what is *that*?"

"*That* is Biscuit." I eye the small game hanging from the tree. "What are you doing?"

"Looks like a sorry mutt to me," he grunts, stepping closer. "Where's your rifle? What if you ran into a bear? Or worse—man?"

"You're a man. Besides, I have no one left to live for." I take the rope from my basket, but Gideon snatches it gently from my hand and begins tying it to the same branch he tied the hare to. He gestures for me to pass the basket to him so he can tie it up as well.

"I could say the same," Gideon mutters. "So don't speak such things."

Shame fills me at the thought of his beautiful wife dying during childbirth while he fought a war he barely returned from.

"You're leaving meat for them," I say softly. "Why?"

We've never discussed me leaving the family bread. Just nodded over trades—bread for fish, small game. He must've seen me leaving loaves here before.

"The same reason you provide them bread, I suppose. They don't deserve to go hungry because their man chose the wrong side." He steps away from the tree.

"He didn't choose the wrong side," I protest. I don't rightly know if that's true, but I don't like hearing it, be that as it may.

Gideon growls and steps past me. "Come on, I'm walking you home."

Once again shame fills me. I'm certain he feels if he'd been here maybe Lily and the baby would have lived. In truth, there was nothing that could be done.

"Why'd you name that mutt Biscuit? What kind of name is that anyhow?" He leads the way through the trail, his heavy footfalls breaking twigs and crushing dried leaves.

"I happen to love biscuits. Especially with jam, or honey, or gravy."

He huffs. "I mean for a dog."

"He snuck into my cabin and helped himself to a pan of biscuits. I thought it fitting." I smile. I can laugh about it now.

"You know the town folk won't go for us feeding the enemy. There's talk of them stealing."

"They don't need to know, besides, I'm certain I know who it is and it's not any one of the Hollis's."

He lifts his hat, runs his fingers through his hair. "I agree, but they could easily find us out. I found out about you, didn't I?"

When we reach my cabin, Gideon opens the door and gestures for me to go inside. I hesitate briefly before stepping over the threshold. Something about the way he stands there, leaning against the frame, thumbs hooked in his suspenders—it makes my heart stutter.

"Aren't you coming in?"

"It wouldn't be proper."

He's come in before, when we've traded.

I cross my arms in front of me. "Why didn't you tell the town I've been leaving bread for the Hollis's?" I feel there's more to his intention than he speaks.

He licks his bottom lip, glances about. The moment feels oddly intimate.

"I told you—Hollis's wife and children don't deserve to go hungry."

Gideon shifts his weight, looks at the floor, then adds, "Truth is...I can't stand the thought of them living out there in tents. It's not right."

I step forward, aching to reach out and touch the man who hides so much behind that hard jaw and rough voice.

He straightens and takes hold of the doorknob. "Now don't be wandering out at night anymore. You hear me?"

I lift my chin. "You are not my husband, sir"

He smirks. "You best be glad I'm not too. I'd bend you over my knee."

"Why you—!"

I march forward, but before I can reach him, he tips his hat and closes the door in my face.

I have one hand on the stack of fabric and one ear on the conversation at the potbelly stove.

"A bag of feed was missing from the Roberts's barn this morning." Marv Clayton states in disgust.

Jonas Billings cuts in, "I hear a pie was taken right off Sheila Brennan's kitchen counter."

"Probably her unruly children," mutters Abe Gibson, who is much younger and more naïve than the men he converses with.

Marv grunts. "Sheriff's got to do something about that Hollis family. Things are getting out of hand." Then he adds, "Says unless there's proof, his hands are tied."

The air is stuffy. Besides the gossip, the only sound is that of floorboards creaking underfoot. I keep my eyes on the muted fabric patterns, fingers brushing over them in consideration.

"We could do some scouting of our own," Jonas says.

A sudden gust of autumn wind rattles the mercantile's wavy glass panes with a tinkling spray of rain.

Abe shifts uneasily, and the floor groans beneath him. "I gotta get back to work, fellas." He pulls his hat further down on his head. "But I can go with you iffen you wanna go on Sunday after church."

"Sounds good."

Marv's husky voice is cut off by Jonas. "Meet at my place. We'll find the proof the sheriff needs."

"See ya Sunday, boys." The bell above the door jingles as Abe slips out into the wind.

"Missus Foster?" I call, peering around the corner of the aisle nearest to me.

The shopkeeper rounds the shelves, her hips broad, gray streaks tucked into her bun. "Did you decide on a pattern, dear?"

"I'm afraid I can't. And I'm getting concerned about the weather. It looks like a storm is rolling in. I think I should come back another time."

"No trouble at all." She takes the bundle as I whistle for Biscuit.

Outside, a fine mist dampens the dirt and perfumes the air with the scent of wet earth. Biscuit trots at my side, ears perked as the clomp of hooves approaches.

Gideon dismounts and walks beside me.

"I left meat for the Hollis's a few days back," he says. "It's still there."

"I saw. I took bread on Monday."

"It's still there too."

Leaves crunch underfoot, and the trees shelter us from the drizzle. His brow furrows.

"I rode on the outskirts of the Hollis's camp. They're skin and bones, Hattie. They won't make it through the winter in those tents."

I sigh. "I was just at the mercantile and overheard Marv Clayton, Jonas Billings, and Abe Gibson discussing the family—accusing them of stealing. They plan to ride out there on Sunday after church to '*find proof.*' They say the sheriff won't do anything without it."

Gideon grunts. "I'd bet my homestead it's Rutger Thomas. The man's a lazy drunk. He's been caught stealing before."

I nod. "That's my thoughts as well."

Wind shakes the tree limbs, and Gideon's horse tosses her head.

Unsure if I should share my thoughts, I hesitate but then speak before fear can stop me. "I have some money saved. It's not a lot, but I'd like to use some of it to purchase provisions for the Hollis family. I'll have to go to another town so as not to raise suspicions."

He narrows his eyes. "How will you do that? You don't have a horse, or wagon."

"I have a sled and two feet."

Truth is, I don't even know which way to go. But I won't let him know that.

He stops, reins in hand. "That is ridiculous. You can't be venturing out alone."

I place my hands on my hips. How dare he tell me what I can and can't do. This man is becoming a thorn in my boot. "And why not?"

He scrubs his hand down his face. "It's not safe." He stomps a foot. "I'll take you. I have a horse and a decent size wagon. When do you want to leave?"

Do I want to be beholden to this man? Not really. But this is for a good cause.

"Tomorrow at first light."

"Fine," he says in clear agitation then proceeds to continue walking.

Reluctantly, we will be working together to help this family. Whether we survive one another in the process remains to be seen.

As we leave Crystal Springs with the wagon loaded full—everything we could pay for or trade—rain gives way to snow. It's been falling steady since we left Juniper the morning before, and now it's turning wet and heavy.

The trip has been long, cold, and soaked straight through, but I keep my thoughts on the Hollis family, huddled in those thin tents. At least I'll return to four sturdy walls and a fire. They've got none of that.

Hours pass. The silence should be companionable, but it's not. Gideon, who's barely said five words since we left, keeps shifting in his seat. Jittery. Uncomfortable.

I sigh and turn to look up at him. "Do you think maybe you could…"

But I stop. Despite the cold, wind, and blowing snow, he's sweating. Beads cover his brow. His jaw clenched tight.

I gasp. "Do you have a fever?" I reach up to feel his face, but he flinches away from me.

"No," he growls.

"What is it?"

"It's nothing." His voice is low—flat.

I cross my arms, lips pressed tight. Fine. Let him stew in misery.

As we continue to bump our way down the trail, we come to a place in the road I recall from our trip to town when we stopped to let the horse rest and drink from the creek. I had noted an abandoned shack through the trees. The wood was weathered, and grass had grown up around the door. Still, it's shelter.

"Can we stop here? I think moving our bodies will do us good. Warm us up."

In truth it's probably warmer under the hides that cover us, but I need to distance myself from this broody man fidgeting beside me.

Gideon grunts and guides the horse off the trail and closer to the narrow creek.

I hop down from the wagon and stretch my aching legs. Running a gloved hand down along the mare's nose, I murmur, "How you doing, girl?"

A thud and sudden yelp break through the quiet.

Gideon's on the ground.

He's flat on his back, one leg stretched out, his hand gripping his thigh. His face is twisted in pain, teeth clenched so hard it looks like they might crack.

I rush to his side, kneeling beside him. "What is it? What can I do?"

"My bag," he gasps. "Behind my seat. Get the Laudanum."

I scramble to the wagon and fumble through the supplies. His bag is there. I open it to find the medicine—and a bottle of whiskey. That surprises me more than it should.

"Here." I put the medicine bottle to his lips. He drinks, then lets his head fall back onto the snow-soaked earth, chest heaving.

I scan our surroundings in desperation.

The shack.

I must get him inside. "I'll be right back," I say as I run for the building, not giving him the opportunity to protest being left there in the cold wet dirt alone.

The door creaks open easily. Inside, it's empty. Just a stone hearth, bare floorboards, and two small windows letting in the gray light of afternoon.

It isn't much.

But it'll have to do.

The fire crackles as I lay another piece of wood on the flames. Once Gideon fell asleep on the makeshift bed that I made him from the hides, I went searching for wood. The room has warmed up nicely and I've long shed my coat.

Biscuit lays near the hearth, head on his paws, staring into the fire with those pitiful eyes of his.

Gideon stirs and grunts. When he opens his eyes, he looks around in bewilderment. Then he lifts the hide and peers down at his bare skin.

"Your clothes were wet. I had to get them off, so you don't catch a chill." I don't mention what I saw while undressing him. It's not my business.

His eyes flick to me, then to where his clothes lie over the hearth.

He nods and relaxes.

"Would you like some bread and jerky?" I set a tin plate of food beside him.

"My horse."

"I fed and watered her. She's tied to a tree behind the house, safe from the wind."

He props himself up on one elbow and winces, then bites into the jerky. "Whiskey." His voice is gravelly.

I hand him the bottle from his bag. He takes a long pull then offers it to me. "I think after all the work you've put in, you deserve a drink."

I think of dragging his body in here, undressing him, seeing to the horse, and making a fire. "I suppose you're right." I smile and take a swig, feeling the burn in my throat. It spreads, warming my chest.

"I'm naked," he states, taking a bite of bread and reaching for another drink of whiskey. He passes the bottle back to me.

"I told you—your clothes were wet." I smile faintly. "Besides, it's not as if I've never seen a naked man before."

He tips the bottle back again. "Looks like we're staying the night here." He glances around. The sun set about an hour ago, and the only light is the flickering of the fire.

"Yeah," I whisper, breathing through the spicy drink.

"You did good, Hattie." He takes another bite of jerky and watches me.

I'm noticing the effects of the liquor. My body feels light—loose. I smile, surprised at how natural this all seems—how natural *he* seems. His arms and shoulders are strong, and I find myself missing James's arms holding me. My eyes drift to Gideon's chest.

He clears his throat.

I jerk my gaze away, horrified. "I'm so sorry." I thrust the bottle back to him and move away, heat rising in my cheeks.

He grins, a big beautiful smile.

I cover my face and chuckle.

But then his smile falters. "The scars."

My heart clenches. I recall what I saw—burns, whip marks, the raw wound on his thigh. I'd wept quietly while undressing him, though he hadn't known it.

"You don't have to tell me," I say gently. "The war was hard. I don't want you reliving it."

I turn back to the fire and stoke it with a stick, the crackling wood echoing between us.

"I live with it every day." He pauses, his voice quieter now. "And I suppose to know why I'm helping the Hollis's...you need to know the truth about me."

I move closer, giving him my full attention. "Go on."

He chuckles and hands me the bottle. "You better take a few more gulps of this."

"After Lee surrendered," he begins, "I chose to help wounded Confederate soldiers. Some were boys. Some were enslaved men forced to fight. None of them had any business being there."

I nod. I won't judge something I have no real knowledge of.

"They caught us. Called us traitors. Imprisoned us. Tortured us." His eyes flick to mine. "I was shot trying to run. Shrapnel's still in my leg, and it flares something fierce in the cold, especially if I sit too long." He glances down. "As you learned."

My eyes blur. "I'm so sorry."

"There's nothing for you to be sorry about. It's not your fault."

"Life can be so cruel," I whisper.

His smile returns, soft this time. "Yes. As we've both come to understand."

He surprises me by lifting his hand and wiping a tear from my cheek with his thumb.

"Now, why don't you have another drink with me...and tell me something good."

I giggle and nod. "All right."

The sun is out today, and the temperature is much warmer. Best of all, Gideon appears to be back to himself. Actually, better, considering something has changed between us. There's a lightness between us. He's talked the whole way back to Juniper, telling me stories of the war, his childhood, and the best way to skin a rabbit. I've listened and asked questions when appropriate, truly thankful for the friendship that's seemed to bloom between us after yesterday. We now share something special, something just between him and me.

After a long conversation with the Hollis's about why we were eager to help them, they accepted our offer. You'd have thought it was Christmas with the excitement of the children over nails, canvas, rope, beans, flour, onions, salt, and coffee.

When we'd told the shopkeeper in Crystal Springs why we were making these purchases, he threw in some dried apples and a peppermint stick for each child.

Their eyes are as big as teacups when I pull the brown paper wrapped in twine from my bag.

"Is it all right, Ma?" one of the boys asks.

Temperance Hollis smiles. "It's not every day such lovely children get peppermint sticks. Yes, it's all right. And I'll make us a nice pie with the apples." She looks to Gideon. "Won't you and Missus Walker join us for supper?"

I give him a smile and a slight nod.

"We'd be obliged," he says.

Gideon smacks his hat on his leg then places it on his head. "What do you say, Hollis, you and me make a plan for this shelter of yours while these ladies prepare the meal?"

I chop onions while Temperance mixes dough for biscuits. "You two are sweet on each other." An amused smile plays on her lips.

My eyes grow big and I stop cutting. "What? Oh, no. We're just friends, that's all."

She chuckles. "So you say."

I think back over the last twenty-four hours and recall the times I'd felt that familiar flutter in my belly but quickly brushed it away. Oh dear, does my face reveal more than it should?

"Truly, we're just friends."

Temperance nods and clenches her lips as if fighting back a retort.

Gideon and I are honestly just friends. That's all.

We depart the Hollis camp with plans for Gideon and I to return the next day with his tools to help get started on the building of a shelter to see the family through the winter.

"I'm so thankful we can help the Hollis's."

We pull up to my cabin. "Me too," Gideon replies.

I move to step down, but he lays his hand on my arm. "Let me help you."

I don't need help. I know that. He knows that. But I stay put until he comes around and reaches for me.

"I'll see you in the morning, Hattie Mae."

Gideon hands me my carpet bag he just pulled from behind the seat. "Good night."

I wake to a loud crash. Feeling disoriented, I'm trying to figure out where I am. Am I dreaming? Then I realize Biscuit's barking. There's several thuds then the sound of the dry wood of my front door splintering. Someone's just kicked it in. Glass shatters and tin clinks and bangs.

I crouch between the bed and the wall. I'm not a praying woman, but I'm praying now. If there is a God, I beg him to keep me safe. Crying, I pray Biscuit hushes lest whoever is out there hurts him. Then boots stomp across my bedroom floor. The quilt is snatched off my bed and I clench my eyes close and bite into my nightgown where I've balled it into my fist.

The boots make their way around the bed where a rough hand snatches me up and pulls me to my feet. The man's face is covered with a bandana but when he speaks there's no mistaking who it is.

Marv Clayton.

"Look what I got, boys." He laughs, dragging me out to the other room. I see another man, face covered, stop mid pour of flour or sugar. It's hard to tell in the dark. But it's clear based on height and size that the other men are Abe and Jonas.

"Please, no!" I shout to the one I believe to be Abe pouring out my goods. "It's all I got."

Marv's hand strikes my face. "Shut up, traitor."

My cheek stings and the sharp tang of iron blooms on my tongue.

He takes hold of my hair and I sob. Fear courses through me. Fear of what they'll do to me. Fear of how I'll replace what they're destroying.

"Please." I beg again.

"I said shut up." Marv shoves me to the ground and a burst of pain explodes from my thigh where his boot has just landed.

Abe calls, "Please don't hurt her. You said we were just going to scare her."

Another blow from Marv's boot strikes my bottom and another slam to my head. Everything goes fuzzy.

I wake to the moon bathing Biscuit in light. He's curled up by my side, peering at me with his sad drooping eyes. Only now do I know he is sad. His whimpers break my heart.

"It's all right, boy," I choke out.

His ears perk up, and he licks my face. I attempt to smile but my lip splits open and begins to bleed. Pushing up onto my elbow, I wipe my mouth with the back of my other hand.

"Hattie Mae!" Gideon runs in through the open doorway. He stops and glances around before rushing to me. "What happened?"

"Marv Clayton."

When Gideon lifts me up, I look down where the flour and sugar have been spilled onto the kitchen floor. The words *Traitor's Bread* are spelled out into the dry goods.

"They know we're helping the Hollis's."

Gideon guides me to the table. "I'll deal with them later. Right now, I'm taking care of you."

"I'll have to order glass and will need to build you a new door. You can't stay here like this, so get your things together, you're coming home with me." He's angry, but I know it's not directed at me.

"I promise, I'm all right. A few bruises and a broken lip won't kill me. I can stay here." I do my best to reassure him.

His tone is stern and even. "You don't even have a front door. You're coming home with me."

I know there's no persuading him and truth is, I don't know if Marv and the others will return, so I pack my bag. "Come, Biscuit."

I look to Gideon daring him to contradict me. "Biscuit is coming."

His expression softens and the corner of his mouth tips up. "Of course."

At Gideon's table, he passes me a plate of green beans with onions, salt pork, and corn bread. I take a bite. Then another.

"I'm not much of a cook, but I did learn a thing or two from the freedmen."

Not much of a cook? I've never tasted anything so wonderful in my life. "Gideon. This is the best meal I've ever eaten."

He pours water from a pitcher he filled from his pump. "The trick is seasonings, onions, lard, and slow cooking. At least that's what Ephraim and the boys told me." He grins and shrugs.

"I don't know who Ephraim is, but he knew what he was talking about." I take another bite and close my eyes, savoring every bit of goodness.

"I should have been there." Gideon's voice breaks the silence.

"There's no way you could have been there."

He lays down his fork and swipes his palm over his face. Placing a hand on his knee he stares at me. It's intense, as if he's angry but I know it's not at me.

I set my fork on my plate and reach for his hand. "There's nothing you could have done. But, it's the middle of the night, why'd you come?"

He takes my face in his hand. "Something just told me to go check on you. I couldn't sleep until I did. I'm sorry, Hattie. I'm so sorry." He draws me in and kisses the corner of my lip, the side that isn't injured. "I'm so sorry."

"It's all right." I kiss him back as heat builds between us.

His lips move to my cheek and down my neck.

"Oh, Gideon." I want him. I need him.

He lifts me from the chair with surprising ease, as if carrying me is as natural as breathing. In his arms, nothing exists beyond the space between us—only the steady beat of his heart beneath my cheek, grounding me.

He carries me to his bed tucked in the corner of the room, where the firelight dances over the walls and shadows fall soft. There, we melt into one another, as if we were always meant to fit this way—flesh to flesh, wound to wound, soul to soul.

Heat blooms between us, slow and certain—not rushed but rising, like spring after a long, bitter winter. His hands explore me with reverence, learning the curve of my waist, the softness of my belly. My fingers trace the planes of his chest, the strength in his shoulders, the roughness of a life survived.

Our bodies move together like prayer—aching and sacred. The grief, the fear, the rage I've carried since James left for war—all of it spills free beneath the tenderness of Gideon's mouth, the surety of his touch. He doesn't rush. He doesn't take. He gives. And I receive him like I'm remembering how.

I've hidden so much beneath strength and silence. Wounds no one's ever seen. But he doesn't flinch. He doesn't ask. He just holds.

And that's when I know—I don't have to carry it alone anymore.

This shouldn't feel so right. But it does. His body, though unfamiliar to the touch, feels like coming home.

When the last shiver fades and the stillness settles, he holds me close, his arms strong and sure. I breathe in the scent of the fire smoke, his skin, and something sweeter still—peace.

And for the first time since James left, I fall asleep utterly satisfied—in body, in heart, and in spirit.

After breakfast, Gideon reluctantly left me at my cabin to clean up the destruction of last night while he headed into town for supplies to temporarily cover the windows and front door. We told Jed and Temperance we'd be out to their camp this morning and we still intend to be there, albeit late. Marv Clayton and his cronies won't stop us.

Gideon left me with his rifle with the demand to use it on anyone who stepped onto my property wrong. I gave my promise, then he kissed me tenderly and left.

It's strange how I can feel hope amongst this mess as I sweep up the last of the dry goods from the floor.

When Gideon returns, my stomach flutters and I move to greet him at the door. But his face doesn't return my smile. He appears...distressed.

"What's the matter?" I shade my eyes from the sun and watch as he ties his horse to the post.

He motions for us to move into the house. "The sheriff has Hollis."

"What?" I blink. "Whatever for?"

"They're saying he was found with stolen goods. A bag of feed conveniently labeled with the Roberts name, a pie plate with the Brennan family crest engraved on the bottom, and a pearl handled gun belonging to Marv himself."

Anger surges through me like fire and I begin to pace. "Now you know as good and well as I do that it was Clayton."

"And you know as well as I that the sheriff would need proof. The items were found in Hollis's possession."

"They had to have been planted. This is all Marv's doing."

"Will you please sit down? You're making me nervous," he says, lowering into a chair, motioning for me to sit, then folds his arms tight across his chest.

I let out a sharp laugh—bitter and dry. "Oh, they sure had their fun last night, didn't they? Coming here destroying my home, laying their filthy hands on me, then planting *stolen* goods on Jed Hollis before calling on the sheriff."

Marching to my bedroom, I grab a shawl and sling it around my shoulders. When I return, I'm heading for the door.

"What are you doing?" Gideon rises.

"I'm going into town to do something about this."

"What exactly do you think you're going to do?" he growls. His hands rest on his hips.

"I'll talk to the sheriff and tell him he's got the wrong man. I'll tell him what Marv and the others did to me." I gesture around the room. "And to my cabin."

"Hattie Mae, be sensible."

I gasp, stunned.

"Telling on those men will bring you more harm. You know Marv's wife is the sheriff's sister. And you have no proof that Hollis didn't take those things."

I step toward him, pointing to my bruised cheek and split lip. "Look at my face." Then I jab my finger at the open space that used to be my front door. "Look at my home. How do you expect me to be sensible about this?"

"You don't think I'm angry too?" He leans into me, voice rising. "You don't think I don't want to go round those bastards up and teach them what it feels like to hurt someone who can't fight back? To tar and feather them for what they did to you? I do. But we must be smart about this."

Smart. Ha.

I let out a huff—part chuckle. "No. I think you're scared of them. Just admit it. You're afraid."

He straightens. His face goes hard. He nods, but not in agreement, in realization. Like he's just seen something in me he didn't want to see.

I suddenly feel small and want to take back my words, but I can't. My pride won't allow it.

He lifts a hand as though he's about to speak, wags a finger, then drops it. Without a word, he turns, walks out the door, unhitches his horse and rides off in a cloud of dust.

The silence he leaves behind is deafening.

And then everything in me boils over—the rage at Marv Clayton for what he and his boys have done, the injustice of Jed Hollis being jailed, the way I lashed out at Gideon as though he were the enemy. The fear of what's next. Everything.

I let out a scream so raw it tears at my throat.

And then I crumble to the floor, sobbing, heaving, broken, spent.

As I lie in a heap, a thought comes to me. *Kindness.* And just like that, an idea forms.

Stepping into the mercantile, I'm quickly met with a deafening silence as the sheriff, Marv, Jonas, and Abe stand around the pot belly stove, their smiles falling. Abe shuffles his feet and looks away. Marv stares at me with defiance and the sheriff straightens.

"Hattie Mae? What happened to you?" he asks, shock on his face.

I smile as sweetly as I can muster. "Sheriff, the bread's still warm. I thought you might be hungry." I hand him a small loaf wrapped in a gingham cloth and tied with twine. "About Jed Hollis, I reckon you've got a choice to make. I hope, for everyone's sake, it's the right one."

Calm and steady I turn to Marv and hand him a loaf. He stares at it. The sheriff nudges him and he takes it. I then hand a loaf each to Jonas and Abe, who cautiously take them.

Abe's eyes are filled with regret. "Hattie Mae..." He swallows hard, but the words don't come easy. It's clear he's been wrestling with something—perhaps all morning.

A bit too late for that.

I look the men in the eye. "Don't take my kindness for weakness. Have a wonderful day, fellas." With my now empty basket looped over my arm, I turn and walk away.

Missus Foster is standing at the end of the aisle. She gasps when she sees me. "Hattie Mae, my dear, what happened to your face?"

I grin. "Good day, Missus Foster."

Behind her, a few more faces peek out from between shelves, silent and uncertain. No one moves.

Not yet.

The bells above the door chime behind me.

Eating a slice of bread with jam at my table, I sit looking out on this warm autumn day pondering what I'm going to do about my front door before nightfall.

Biscuit snoozes beside me. He's the only one I can count on I think as I take another bite. Then, his ears perk up.

"What is it boy?"

He jumps to his feet and moves to the door.

I follow him as he begins barking. It's Jillian Bixby and her husband Loren with their team and wagon.

"Hush, Biscuit."

"Hattie Mae." Jillian waves as they make their way into my yard.

I step out to greet them and the woman jumps from the wagon almost before her husband brings it to a stop.

"Oh, Hattie Mae, your face." She takes hold of my shoulders.

I think of how the bruising on my thigh and bottom hurts worse than my face looks.

She pulls me in for a hug. At first, I'm unsure what to do with my arms as I'm caught off guard, but then I wrap them around her.

"We heard what happened," she says pulling away. She gestures to the wagon as Loren grabs a sack of flour and lifts it over his shoulder.

"How? What?" I'm so confused about what's happening.

"All right if I set this inside?" he asks.

"Uh, yes, of course." I shake my head and look to Jillian for an explanation.

She takes hold of my arm and ushers me back inside where we sit at the table as Loren brings in a sack of sugar.

"Abe said you took bread to him and the others this morning...your kindness made him feel so guilty he confessed to the sheriff what he and Marv and Jonas had done to you. He also confessed that the stolen goods found at the Hollis camp had been planted by Marv."

"Folks didn't know what to make of it at first," she adds. "Some didn't want to believe it. But once Gideon brought Missus Hollis and the children into town, and folks saw them up close—hungry, scared, with nothing but the clothes on their backs...it changed something."

"Gideon told Missus Foster to give the family whatever they needed and put it on his bill. I was in the store when he brought them in. I was so upset to hear the news about you and asked him if there was anything you needed. He said you needed dry goods and asked if Loren would mind coming out and building you a door and putting canvas over the windows until new ones came in."

She looks at the already covered windows.

"Yes, I already did those," I say quietly at the thought of Gideon thinking of me. Shame creeps up my cheeks.

Jillian pats my hand. "Well now, Marv and the others are in jail, and the town has rallied around the Hollis family."

"What do you mean?"

"Oh yes, everyone set out with wagons full to help Gideon and Jed Hollis build that family a proper cabin." She shakes her head. "Maybe it was guilt. Maybe shame. Maybe your bravery just gave 'em permission to do the right thing."

When Loren has the new door hung, he helps me, Biscuit, and Jillian into the wagon and we make our way over to the Hollis's to help with the build.

Temperance Hollis strikes the triangle shaped dinner bell calling the men to eat.

My stomach twists and turns at the thought of seeing Gideon, not knowing how he'll receive me.

I watch him as he washes his hands at the basin and runs his wet fingers through his hair. Then he looks up and notices me noticing him. Swallowing past the lump in my throat, I take a deep breath and make my way to him.

My hands smooth over my apron.

Dirt clings to his boots.

"I—I just want to apologize for what I said this morning. It—It was wrong, and I'm truly sorry." I continue to stare at his boots while wringing my hands. My eyes move to one of his suspender straps. "I hope you can find it in your heart to forgive me." His collar is damp from him scrubbing his face with the cool water. "I'm so sorry." A tear runs down my warm cheek and my focus goes back to his boots.

Gideon takes hold of my chin and gently lifts my face to look at his. "There's nothing for you to be sorry about. Nothing for you to apologize for. No, I'm not a coward, but I didn't see a way to make any of the wrongs right again. But you—when I heard what you did and how it got Abe to confess, it gave me the courage to take this family into town and help the people to see how their prejudice was hurting innocent folks. Making them look into the faces of the Hollis children and seeing their intolerance had consequences. I'm the one who needs to apologize to you for doubting anything could be done. I'm sorry for not listening to you. You had the answer all along. With bread. And courage. And a kindness so steady it made the town listen."

This town hasn't been the same since that day last fall when the folks rallied around the Hollis's and built them a real home. Mister

Foster offered the empty building next door to the mercantile for me to start a true bakery rather than using my baking to barter out of my home. I insisted on making payments to him until the building was paid in full, so I'd own it myself and he agreed.

"No interest, though. The Bible forbids it."

We shook on it, and then Gideon immediately placed an order with a local carpenter for signage. He insisted it be a surprise.

"It's up." Gideon pokes his head in the door of the bakery.

I wipe my hands on my apron. "I'm coming."

Excitement fills me as I run out into the street and look back at the building. Gideon puts his arm around me. "What do you think, sweetheart?"

The sign reads, *The Bread Keeper—Hattie Mae's Bakery.*

"Oh." Tears well and I squeeze him tight to my side. "I love it."

He places a kiss on the top of my head. "Only the best for my beautiful, brave, *kind* wife."

About Amanda Speights

Historical Western Romance author, Amanda Speights, weaves spicy tales of resilient women and bold adventures from her home at the foot of America's Mountain where she lives with her husband and daughter. Her passion for storytelling shines through her work, honoring the Old West's amorous spirit. Amanda invites her readers to saddle up and journey through love stories that are as enduring as the Rocky Mountains themselves

Her debut novel, "Love's Arrival," is the first book in the Laurel Springs series, set in the Colorado Territory during the late 1800s. Amanda loves engaging with her readers and offers a newsletter, which can be found at www.AmandaSpeights.com, to keep fans informed about her latest releases and book news. Followers can also connect with her on Instagram at @AmandaJSpeights.

Amanda divides her time between crafting her latest historical romance, homeschooling her daughter, and immersing herself in period fiction that spotlights formidable women.

For more information about Amanda and updates, go to: https://amandaspeights.com/

Cassoulet

SARAH BRANSON

January 2388

Mama is dying.

I make this phrase into a mantra as I run, saying each word as each foot hits. *Mama*, thump, *is*, thump, *dying*, thump. The phrase repeats in my head and on my lips as the kilometers click by. Is it the phrase that chills me or the icy January breeze blowing down from the north? Either way, I push myself harder. Mama is dying.

I can barely believe those words. And yes, I get it. The woman is two months from her ninety-first birthday, and since just after New Year's, she has been sleeping more, eating less, and can no longer stand on her own. If someone else had told me their elderly mother was showing those signs, I'd cluck sympathetically and say something about "how remarkable for you all that you've had her here for so very long."

But it's not someone else. It's Mama: Miriam Grey Keaton Bosch...and maybe Richmond? I'm not sure whether she ever changed her name when she and Jace married twenty years ago.

She is...what, a celebrity? Maybe. An institution? That might be closer. Here on Bosch, a mid-sized island set off the northeast coast of the Central Continent in New Earth, home to the fiercest, smartest, and most delightful people on the planet, I would wager there isn't a soul over the age of fifteen who doesn't know her or of her.

She was a midwife for years, serving the birthing families of Bosch. And beyond that she has been a powerhouse in the community, always ensuring those in need were tended to and nurtured. I was one of those she nurtured. She and my late papa—*the* Teddy Bosch, beloved master commander of the Bosch Pirate Force for thirty-five years before he retired—took me in over forty years earlier when I slipped the bonds of my enslavement and hid on Teddy's air vessel.

Teddy brought me to Mama, the one who saw the damage inside me, who bathed and nurtured the angry, broken, frightened young woman I was, who held me in the bath as I wept the years of pain and suffering out. She made sure that Peter, Paul, and Mimi—the bio kids, I call them—the children born to her and Papa, accepted me as part of the family, a family more loving to me during the first month I knew them than the one I was born into in the North Country. Mama, who cared for me as a midwife through each of my pregnancies, even the last, which ended in heartbreak so long ago. Mama, my confidant, friend, and mentor, the lodestar of my life. How can that person just disappear? How can Mama die?

Less than a year ago, we celebrated her ninetieth. She walked in using the cane decorated with sparkles and ribbons by her great grandchildren and wearing the exquisite white-and-gold outfit Mimi gave her, laughing and waving at her audience. Walk... She practically danced in as family and friends cheered her and sang the birthday song. It was a raucous and joyous day. Less than a month ago, we were gearing up to celebrate another Winter Gifting Holiday, Mama assigning tasks and prepping all her usual celebratory season dishes. Less than a week ago, "that new doctor"—Mama's title not for the female replacement of the family physician who saw Miriam and Teddy and the rest of us through so much, but the replacement's replacement—came by to see her at the family's request.

Mama had protested that she didn't need Dr. Ramirez to examine her. She only capitulated when Peter, her oldest at sixty-six, put on his patented errant teenager look. "Peter, you are far too old to make that face just to get your way," Miriam scolded.

He had wheedled, "And you are far too old to refuse a simple exam when the good doctor has come all this way."

Mama's right eyebrow came up. "She lives three blocks away, Peter. Don't try that with me."

Peter grinned his still-boyish grin. "Well, either way, she's here now, so..."

"All right. Fine. But she's just going to tell you that I'm old and running out of steam." Mama lifted her hands in mock surrender.

Dr. Ramirez waited with her stethoscope until receiving Mama's nod of consent. "Well, Miriam. Let's see if our diagnoses match."

A half-hour later, the doctor was sitting in the living room, where the bio kids and I sat with Jace, looking out at the cold, gray

January as a depressing mix of rain and snow spattered the ground beyond the big windows. "Well, I have to concur with Miriam's diagnosis. While I did feel a possible mass in her belly, which could be significant, she has decided that at her age, the cure would be worse than the disease, and she only wants comfort measures."

For a few moments we all just sat in silence, processing what that meant. Jace broke the stillness when he stood, shook Dr. Ramirez's arm, and said, "I know Miriam appreciates you coming by. We all do." Then he looked at us four. "I'm gonna sit with her," he announced and went to the back bedroom to be with his wife.

Paul cleared his throat and asked what we were all wondering: "How long?"

Ramirez shrugged. "A couple weeks? A month? It's hard to say, not knowing exactly what we are dealing with. Also, your mama is made of sturdy stuff and has a stubborn streak, so we have to take those things into account."

Mimi looked stunned. "I need to let the kids know. They'll want to come over."

"We should take turns staying over if Jace is okay with that," Paul said, and Peter nodded in agreement.

They all pulled out their calendars on their devices, and I pulled out mine. The rush of acceptance and inclusion that permeates my time with these three and their families flooded into me more strongly than it had for years. That family taught me what love, trust, and loyalty mean. We will be there for Mama.

I strip my shoes and outerwear off in the back entry, the heat of the house turning on my sweat as if it's a faucet. A thump and grunt from the hall catch my attention. Jace has Mama in his arms like she's his bride. Given that Jace isn't that much younger than Mama, I have to smother the urge to rush over and help him. But I exercise patience, not my strongest trait, and see that he is not struggling. In fact, the two are whispering and giggling, and I realize, she still *is* his bride. He carries her to the front room as I slip upstairs to shower and dress for my first day with my mama, who is dying.

Washed and changed, I survey the situation. Jace has carried Mama from the bedroom and settled her into the big, upholstered chair she loves most. Now he is in the study writing on the memoir he has been working on for the past year. I brew a pot of tea and start to pour.

"Milk and sugar as usual?" I call to Miriam.

"Yes, please, dear." Her voice has a distinct quaver to it.

A few moments later, I say, "Here we go," as I slide the tray with its two remaining cups onto the center table, having taken Jace's to him in the study. After stirring Mama's to cool it, I hand it to her. Her hand shakes a bit as she takes it, and the milky, tan liquid splashes onto her robe. "Oops, here, let me." I stabilize the cup with my hand, helping her lift it to her lips before placing it back on the tray.

Unruffled, she smiles. "I've been thinking. I'll be needing more help as I journey to the end."

The end. The words are a stab to my belly, but Mama does not need to comfort me, so I pull a deep breath in, blink several times, and push a stray wisp of silver hair out of her face, tucking it neatly behind her ear. "We will all help...." Then, because I can't help it, I add, "I don't really want the journey to end."

Her face curves into her familiar, gentle smile. "Oh, my darling, all journeys must come to an end. I'm sorry I won't get to see how everyone's story plays out, but I am looking forward to seeing what comes next for me. And I'm tired. It's time. More tea, please."

This time I hold the cup, bringing it to her lips; she sips once and then twice. "Perfect. Now then, I have a job for you."

This pulls a laugh from me. "This had better not be the same job Papa had for me."

Mama giggles as well. "Oh, no, dear, I'm almost ninety-one. I don't need any help getting to the finish line." She looks at me, face serious now, her deep brown eyes clear and acute since she had her cataracts removed ten years ago. They hold my eyes. "I need you to take over one of my jobs."

Jobs? Mama was a midwife for her adult life. She officially retired close to twenty years ago, though she worked with student midwives until she turned eighty. I wrinkle my brow. "I don't think I'm cut out to be a midwife, Mama."

"Oh, definitely not. Your strengths lie elsewhere. It's just..." She pauses, reaching for my hand. "I won't be around for the next Winter Gifting holiday, and I need someone to make the holiday cassoulet."

"What?" Thoughts whirl in my brain as I attempt to envision a holiday without Mama, her chair sitting empty at the table, the house, usually festooned with decorations, drab and dull. How could there even be a holiday without Mama?

And her cassoulet, a rich, steamy dish filled with beans, duck, pork, and sausage. It's traditional. She's made it every year that I can recall; even when she was out all night at a birth, she was still able to put it together somehow. Another thought lunges forward: *You can't do that, Kat.* I can't disagree with that statement. I repeat it aloud: "I can't make that, Mama. I don't have the talent for making something like a cassoulet. I wouldn't know where to start."

"Nonsense, Kat Wallace. You've cooked for me and for your children for years." She squeezes my hand.

She isn't wrong. My children have never gone hungry. I can roast meats and vegetables. In Edo, I mastered the art of steaming rice and grilling fish, along with making a decent miso soup. My baked potatoes are perfect—never mealy. And I have a great fish stew recipe. But that's where my skills stop. "Mama, you know Matty is the one that brings daring and imagination to the kitchen. I think that's why the kids were set on him before I was." I chuckle, remembering their faces at the first meal he made with their help.

Mama puts an age-spotted hand on my arm. "Your Matthieu is a man of many talents, including cooking. Remember that I told you there was someone out there for you who would love you for all your talents and frailties, not in spite of them." She pauses and giggles like a schoolgirl. "Of course, it doesn't hurt he seems to get more handsome with each passing year."

Now I laugh. "You are not wrong there, Mama."

We chuckle together over my good fortune. Then Mama gives me a stern look. "Now then, we both know you can do whatever you put your mind to. And you are going to make the cassoulet next holiday." Her voice no longer holds any quaver—it is firm and clear. She pats my hand that she still holds. "Now don't worry. I'll tell you what you need to know."

I know when I'm beat. I sigh. "You win. I'll try, Mama."

December 2388

"What is that?" My oldest-by-twenty-minutes son, Kik, leans over and peers at my pan of duck legs and duck breasts as he buses his breakfast dishes on a late December morning.

I'm deciphering my own scribbles as I wait for my oven to get to temperature, so my answer is short. "Duck."

There's a frown in his voice. "Sure, but what is it swimming in?"

"Duck fat." I glance over to see whether his reaction is similar to mine when I first learned about how to confit the duck. I see his eyes go wide, and he leans closer to inspect the depths of caramel-colored liquid surrounding my bird pieces.

"That's sort of gross. What's it for?" he asks.

I sigh. "I am not at liberty to say—currently…"

Kik shrugs and heads upstairs, leaving me to confit. It is telling about his upbringing that he just accepts my answer even as a thirty-year-old. He and his husband, Nagai, came in from Edo at the first of the week for the Winter Gifting holiday. They've been married for two years. I like Nagai for many reasons, but lately, especially, because he suggested the two of them move back to Bosch after Kik finishes his doctoral work in Edoan history. He even asked whether the little white house where the kids grew up might be available. Mac, Kik's twin, is coming over from District Four with his wife, Sanchia, and their two kids once school is out to celebrate as well.

I slide the pan of duck and duck fat into the oven and note the time—twenty minutes past ten. The duck will get checked for doneness in three and a-half bells. I put a check mark next to step one and smile, remembering.

"Wait? What? I cover the duck in its own fat? Like, cover-cover?" My voice was incredulous as I sat next to Mama that morning, pen in hand and pad of paper on my lap. I really hate being crap at things, so my tendency is to go overboard with preparation if I'm worried I may not measure up. I picture the family taking a bite of my cassoulet that looks suspiciously like watery, gray stew in my imaginings. They gag, spit, and then rise against me. "*Who do you think you are?*" "*You aren't Mama.*" "*You ruined her most special dish.*"

I have been told I catastrophize things when nervous. Can't imagine where anyone gets that idea.

My brothers and Matty moved Mama's bed to the front room in February. She said she wanted to see the seasons change, so Jace called in the troops, and in an afternoon, the front room became their bedroom. It delighted her to see the late-winter storms blow in and the leafless trees swaying in the wind beyond the windows. By early March, there were buds and leaflets to be enjoyed, and she could see the early spring birds returning to the feeders that the bio kids and I now kept filled for her feathered guests.

Mama was sitting up, propped with pillows surrounding and supporting her, her silver hair spread behind her head like a crown...or halo. Her face looked like a wood carver got carried away, intricately carving a piece of mahogany wood with innumerable deep ridges and grooves overlaid with a spiderweb of tiny marks. The smile she gave me, though, was as gentle and warm as ever, as she leaned forward a bit. "Cover-cover. It's a way of preserving the meat."

"Where did you learn to do this?" I ask as I jotted down, *cover in duck fat.*

Mama leaned back and closed her eyes, the same soft smile still on her now-thinning lips. Watching her, I realized I am now older than she was when I was first deposited into her loving care. This thought was hard to wrap my brain around. She hadn't answered me, and I figured she had gone to sleep.

On that day, several weeks ago, when she told me I was to make the cassoulet, she only got as far as saying that I would need duck, sausage, and a variety of pork before her first visitor had appeared, delighting and tiring her in equal measure. Since then, her cassoulet instructions had slowly trickled out to me during my days at the house. I had just started to rise from my seat when she spoke:

"Remember, I told you Papa and I went to Paris on our honeymoon?" She didn't wait for me to answer. "Well, we didn't just see the city, we borrowed a vehicle and drove all around the countryside. We had stopped for lunch at a small farm restaurant. The woman there served us a green salad with duck confit." She laughed a little. "My French was terrible, and I assumed the duck would be sweet because, to me, *confit* sounded as if it should be like confection or candied, but it was so rich and savory—almost nut-like. I was in heaven, and in my broken French, asked her about it. When she realized I couldn't really understand her words, she took me by the hand and walked me back to the kitchen, showing me the steps in the process and giving me the French words for what she did. At the end she called her son over, who told me in spotless FA, 'Confit meat will last all winter. Plus, it tastes like heaven on earth.'" She paused, still not opening her eyes, then added, "Her name was Madame Gisèle Allard. I liked her." A moment later I heard a small snore, and this time she was well and truly asleep. So, I rose and tucked her blanket around her.

Jace was reading on the sofa and had looked up. "She has been telling lots of old stories lately. Most involve Teddy."

"Is that weird?" I asked.

"Not at all. They had more than forty years together. And Teddy was not only a powerful force but also one helluva a character." Mama's husband chuckled as he said this.

"That he was," I agreed. I hoped Jace knew what a gift he had been to Mama these past twenty years, so I added, "She only chooses to love the best."

Jace refocused on his book, but his smile reflected his pleasure in the comment.

I give a little sigh at the memory, then I decide to focus on my stock, pulling the pan of roasted pork and chicken bones from the second oven. I had scoffed when Matty installed two ovens in what I called "The Project"—his great-grandparents' house that he lovingly restored practically from the studs. After I retired, we moved out to District Four, where Matty grew up and where his family still runs one of Bosch's largest and best vineyards. I was reluctant to leave the little white house near the base where first I, and then we, raised the kids, but once he made good on my request to install a big wooden swing on the front porch looking out west over the vineyard, I wanted to move in immediately. It has become our routine in all but the worst weather to sit together, swinging, holding hands, and watching the sunset as we talk about our days. What we share is not exactly the swashbuckling of our younger adventures but is marvelous nonetheless. Anyway, when he put in a second oven, I told him that was "a foolish waste of space." He had just grinned and said, "You'll like it. You'll see."

As usual, he was right. It's incredibly helpful when cooking for a crowd or even just prepping for a busy week.

The bones are brown and fragrant, and I dump them into my biggest pot with the herbs and aromatics, a chunk of kombu, and lots of water to begin the three-day process of cooking down into a rich stock. I give it a stir and let the fragrance spark my memory.

"I used to only use pork bones until after you moved to Edo. That spring, when your papa and I came out for Grey's birth, your friend Aiko made the ramen broth for you with chicken and pork bones and a piece of kombu. She said it would be the perfect food for after-birth—warm, healing, and would bring in the milk. And she was right." Mama leaned toward me and whispered, "I started making it for my mamas on Bosch after that, and when it came time to prep the holiday cassoulet, I had several jars. So, I used it, and everyone raved. So now that's how I always make it."

I laughed. "Mama, everyone always raves about your cassoulet every damn year."

There was pride and pleasure reflected in her face as she answered, "I know. It's funny how you can give a gift to people and get so much back from the giving."

I sighed at her wisdom and said, "You are a gift to us all that keeps on giving," as I leaned over and kissed her forehead.

Her thin, bony hand wrapped around mine. "Nothing lasts forever, darling. Certainly, I won't."

I knew this. Dr. Ramirez had come by regularly to check in, mostly just to talk, and as the weeks turned to months, she would just shrug when we kids asked the inevitable "How long?" question. She said, "Miriam has always done things her own way. Why should this be any different?"

Ninety-one was a remarkable age to live to—and we celebrated it. Jace and us four kids held a small, quiet party on her birthday just a few days earlier, sharing cake and memories as we all sat on the big bed with her. For the entire week surrounding her birthday, dozens of people dropped over to say hello, wish her well, and tell Miriam—or us if she was resting—just how much she meant to them.

I brought her hand to my lips, placing a kiss between the knuckles. "The love we all have for you will last forever, Mama."

Four days and delicious-smelling nights later, my stock is done and chilled, the collagen in it thickening it like loose aspic, which... Look, I can still learn at fifty-nine. When I started this, I didn't even know what aspic was exactly. I tuck it back into the icebox, then, from the cupboard, pull out the bag of flat, white beans I had Grey bring me from her last mission to the Eastern Continent. I sort them, rinse them, and put them in a big pot, covering them with water to soak.

"Let's keep this recipe just between the two of us for now. I want it to be a surprise for them," she had said.

"But what if I ruin it?" I could hear the wail in my voice.

"My darling, you won't. Cassoulet is very forgiving. But this will be my final chance to leave a holiday gift to them. So, no telling."

I agreed but still had my reservations. My worry kept me awake a few nights. What if my siblings resented that she shared the recipe with me? Normally I wouldn't think that of them, but grief can make people act crazy at times. We didn't talk for quite a while after Papa died because of what I did then. *But this is different*, I try to reassure myself. But is it?

A few weeks ago, I almost broke my promise to Mama and started to message Mimi. Just a quick *Can I run something by you?* My thumb had hovered over the send button as I frowned at the screen. That was when Mama's voice echoed in my head. *"It's a surprise, my darling. Don't tell."*

Sighing, I deleted the message.

"I'll try to do you proud," I whisper to the universe. I'm not sure if I'm addressing Mama or the cassole.

The next day, I head down the cellar to retrieve the sausage I made a few weeks ago. This process has caused me to gain a whole new appreciation for butchers and chefs who make this sort of thing on the regular. Mama's recipe was replete with garlic, and I didn't really believe her when she told me how much. So, my first efforts, while tasty enough, did not make the cut for the cassoulet sausage.

I had come home after my first stay back in January with Mama, and I told Matty about her cassoulet request, which garnered a low whistle from my husband. I admit I then tried to press-gang him into being my ghost-chef.

"No way," he had said, hand up in defense. "Miriam gets what Miriam wants. You have to do it."

I groaned in a sort of mock despair.

"I tell you what." He wrapped me up in his arms. "I'll be your taste tester."

That made me giggle. "That could be a dangerous mission, Colonel."

We kissed and he whispered, "I knew I'd be taking my chances with you. But you are so worth the risk."

The man must have tried four different batches of sausage before holding me by the shoulders, looking me in the eye, and saying, "My love, she said plenty of garlic, so put the damn garlic in."

I knew he was right. "Are these so bad?" I asked, fishing for compliments.

He kissed my forehead. "No. These are delicious. They just aren't cassoulet sausage."

I sighed and nodded. "I'll peel more garlic."

I finally achieved what Matty describes as the perfect French garlic sausage. Now it is time to assemble the cassoulet. Matty buzzes about the kitchen, cleaning up my messes and dipping a spoon into just about everything. I am a fretting, sweaty mess, but I persevere, trying not to imagine the look of horror that may possibly appear on my siblings' faces when they see I have taken over a sacred Mama job.

"You know, maybe I should let Mimi know...," I start.

Matty interrupts, ever my moral compass. "Nope. Miriam said surprise, and she wouldn't have said that if she thought they wouldn't like it."

A resigned sigh escapes my lips. "Yeah. You're probably right."

"Say that again?" I hear the tease in his tone.

I shake the knife I am using at him as I laugh. "I think you are absolutely wrong and can't believe you'd leave me hanging like that."

He laughs as well. "That sounds more like the master commander emeritus I know and love."

It's late by the time I have finished assembling the cassoulet, layering the bean ragout and shredded duck confit and tucking in the sausage on top, and it has baked properly, the surface deeply brown and crusty. The cassole is so big, it won't fit in the icebox. So, I take it out to the screened-in back porch, which in the winter serves as what we term the "big fridge," and set it into the box we have for this purpose. The first winter we moved here, we just set some lasagna on the table on the porch, and in the middle of the night, heard bumps and thumps and discovered a raccoon family feasting away on it; hence, the box. And new screening.

"Let it sit for at least a day and a night, so the flavors meld and it gets happy." It was early April. Grey was over with her family for her birthday and to take some time with Mama, who the grandkids refer to as MamaM, and she looked at me curiously when Mama said this, which to her seemed out of nowhere.

I leaned over to Mama. "I thought this was a secret?"

We had to lean close now to hear her words clearly. "Not from Grey, just from your brothers and sister."

I shrugged. This made no sense, but I was all in. "Got it." Then I turned to my daughter and said, "MamaM has taught me how to make cassoulet. For the holidays. But it's a secret from your aunt and uncles."

Grey grinned and leaned in to murmur to Mama, "That's an excellent secret, MamaM." I was turning away as my granddaughter came toddling into the room, but I could have sworn my mama and my child winked at each other. But I was tired and so was likely mistaken.

The Winter Gifting holiday is upon us. My grandchildren all slept here and are now a-buzz with the presents and treats they received this morning. I am dressed and ready to head to Mama and Jace's place. Well, Jace's place now. I think about this morning—Mac and Sanchia, and Grey and Bran were up early with the kids, along with their uncles Kik and Nagai and their aunt Rini, home on leave. The adult kids all seem well, but there is something subdued that runs just under the surface. I pull the paper card with Mama's picture from when she was, maybe, fifty, that is tucked in my mirror and read it.

Miriam Grey Keaton Bosch Richmond, aka "Mama" and "MamaM" and "Great Grandma" and "Midwife Miriam," died on April 25, 2388, at ninety-one a bit after noon. Her four children and her husband, Jace, were at her side as she slipped peacefully into the unknown, leaving us all a little sadder with her passing but a little better with having known her.

"Anniversaries, birthdays, and holidays will be hard at first," Mama had announced in her raspy whisper one morning around the third week in April. The bio kids and I had tossed our schedule to the side the past couple of weeks because it was clear the end was near. Mama's pronouncement had been the first thing she had said in close to a day.

Mimi answered, "They will be. But you've taught us well, Mama. We'll be there for each other."

Peter, Paul, and I murmured our agreement.

Mama didn't open her eyes, and when she spoke again, I could see the effort it took as she pulled a laborious breath in and the forced out the words, "Good. I love each and every one of you and all your babies and grandbabies." Jace lay next her, holding her lovingly, and she whispered something to him that made him smile.

And that was it. Mama fell asleep and just stopped breathing while Jace held her in his arms and her children held her hands. I had a good six months of being miserable, but then I realized I had a cassoulet to make in just a couple of months, and I'd better get to figuring it out.

Now in the depths of December, we pull up to the brick house I know so well. There is garland and lights draped across the door and the front windows. I carry the cassoulet inside, smiling at the decorations I know so well as I tuck my (hopeful) masterpiece into the oven Jace preheated for me to rewarm. Matty and I are the first ones here, but Mimi and her family arrive as I step out of the kitchen. In my sister's hands are two very familiar-looking pies.

"Is that...?" I start.

Mimi bites her lip, wrinkles her brows, and says, "It is. It's Mama's winter berry pie. She swore me to secrecy."

I am about to answer when the door flies open, and Paul trots in, oven mitts on his hands, holding a pan. "Wellington coming through!"

Mimi and I stare after him but don't get a word out before Peter shows up holding a basket with several loaves of bread.

Mimi is the first to call it: "Mama's sourdough?!"

She's right. The scent is unmistakable.

Peter looks abashed. "She, uh... She gave me her recipe and the starter."

Now Mimi and I start to grin and then laugh. Mimi turns to me. "What about you?"

Paul steps out from the kitchen, his eyes wide. "Cassoulet?"

I point at him. "Wellington?"

A squeal comes from Mimi as the pies and the bread are slipped onto the table. We four reach out for a hand to grasp, then we pull each other into a tearful, chuckling group hug.

I look over Peter's shoulder at the chair where Mama always sat. It isn't empty after all, and it never truly will be. Mama is right here.

About Sarah Branson

Award-winning author Sarah Branson spent nearly thirty years as a midwife before turning to write feminist speculative fiction filled with action, adventure, romance, and resilience. Her debut, *A Merry Life*, won the 2022 Connecticut Adult Fiction Award from the Indie Author Project and launched her four-book *Pirates of New Earth* series. She has since expanded her universe with books for young adult, middle grade, and adult readers, including the upcoming YA novel *For the Love of Glitter* and the adult standalone *North Country*. Sarah lives in Connecticut with her husband.

For more information about Sarah and updates, go to: https://www.sarahbranson.com/

What She Would Have Wanted

CATHELINA DUVERT

Colleen Brown sat in her classroom, elbows on her desk and her head resting in her folded hands. It was 3pm and her students had already gone home. Most of her fellow teachers were gone too. Normally, Colleen would have rushed out of the door at 2:45 when the last class period ended but today, her anticipation to get home was just not there. What was the point of rushing home? To sit beside a mother who no longer recognized her and who sometimes mistook her for a stranger or a thief? The silence in her apartment would be louder than the classroom chaos she'd left behind.

"Hey Colleen." Amber, who the students knew as Ms. Jackson, the science teacher, poked her head through the opened classroom door.

Amber was always Colleen's light in the storm, the one who always helped her reel in her emotions and feelings of panic whenever they overcame her, which happened quite often lately.

She stepped into the room with her bag over her shoulder and her keys in her hand.

Colleen sighed and looked at Amber, her eyes swollen with unshed tears.

"You all right? What happened?" Amber asked, alarmed. She moved closer to Colleen, setting her things down and placing a comforting hand on Colleen's shoulder.

Exasperated, Colleen allowed her words to spill out of her like a pot boiling over, steam rushing out, threatening to burn its closest victim. "I just had my informal observation and it was so horrible. I didn't even have a lesson plan. I spent yesterday evening taking care of my mom. Still, she kept me up half the night and wouldn't cooperate with the health aide this morning. I didn't get a chance to prepare when I got in and I spent the entire day dealing with bad behavior and a meeting with a parent. Some of the kids weren't listening to me during the observation. I didn't even make enough copies of the worksheet. Ugh! I know Ms. Lewis won't hold back her criticisms."

"Stop!" Amber said.

Colleen seemed to jump out of her trance, looking at her friend as if she'd forgotten she was there.

"Good," Amber said. "Now take a deep breath."

With tears in her eyes, Colleen did as she was instructed.

"First of all, no matter how well your lesson goes, Ms. Lewis will always find something to criticize, with or without a lesson plan. One lousy observation after all these years of teaching doesn't change the fact that you are a great teacher."

"I really don't feel like I am," Colleen responded, sinking under the weight of self-doubt. "My slides were all out of order, and some were missing and because of that, I couldn't even get to half the things I wanted to get through. I was so unprepared for today and Ms. Lewis knew it. When she looked at me with that fake smile, I swear I felt like it was my first year teaching all over again. I hadn't felt like that in years."

"Stop beating yourself up! You're still dealing with what happened to your dad no more than a few months ago. And on top of that, you're taking care of your sick mother. You've got to give yourself some grace. Everyone here knows how hard you work with those kids. Just give yourself credit for even being here, girl." Amber sighed. "Listen. Some of us are going out for drinks now. Why don't you join us? Then we can all bad-mouth Ms. Lewis."

Colleen forced a chuckle as she wiped the tears from her eyes. "I can't. It's too last minute to arrange a caretaker for my mom."

Colleen remembered how she and the other teachers always looked forward to those Friday night drinks before a long weekend, claiming they had earned it. Now she couldn't even remember the last time she'd done anything social. Had it really been that long ago? When was the last time she hung out with Amber and the others? Her mother used to admire Colleen's social affability. "I watch you laughing with your friends and it reminds me of the girl I used to be," her mother would tell her quite often in one way or another. "Going out and enjoying yourself just makes life so much better." Now, with her father gone, Colleen couldn't imagine having a fun night out while her mother was home with a stranger in a nurse's uniform.

Amber smiled sympathetically. "How is your mom?"

Colleen threw her head back and looked up to the ceiling before looking back at Amber. "She's not getting any worse, thank God.

But ever since my dad passed away, the whole situation has just gotten so much harder."

Amber reached inside her purse and pulled out a card. "Colleen, I keep telling you. This was the best thing I could have done for my dad and my family. Call the facility. See what they say. They can contact your mom's doctor and insurance company directly. Promise me you'll give them a call sometime this weekend. What's the worst that can happen?"

Colleen took the card from Amber. Gentle Hands Care Facility.

"I can't just dump my mom in a nursing home, Amber. I should be the one who cares for her, not a bunch of strangers. That's what my dad and I tried to do together."

"But he's not here anymore and you can't go on like this by yourself. It's not healthy. You're being too hard on yourself."

Colleen flipped the card in her hands, avoiding Amber's eyes.

"Just think about it, okay?" Amber said.

"Thanks." Colleen now sat with her back slouched and smiled at her colleague and friend.

"You're welcome," Amber responded. She picked up her things to leave. "Well, I hope you do something fun tonight just for you. Even if it means watching something on Netflix to get your mind off of what happened today."

Although Colleen knew she was not likely to do anything fun just for her, she promised she would before Amber left her classroom. As she gathered her own things to exit the building, she looked at the business card once again and a pang of guilt stabbed her stomach. How could she possibly consider a nursing home for her mother when she knew her mother would not have wanted that for herself?

Colleen stepped into the two-bedroom apartment she shared with her mother as the sweet melody of the song *Amazing Grace* greeted her. She placed her bag down on the living room couch and tiptoed towards her mother's bedroom, where she witnessed Marie, the home health aide, singing softly to her sleeping mother, stroking the gray curls of her hair. Yes, the guilt struck her; the last time Colleen was that tender with her mother was when they had first received the diagnosis of dementia from the doctor, before the disease changed who her mother was.

Marie finished her song and carefully stood up so as to not wake up the mother. Upon noticing Colleen, Marie smiled and motioned for them to step outside of the bedroom. She closed the door softly behind her and they walked into the living room.

Colleen knew she was lucky to have Marie care for her mother and often showed her appreciation for the older woman with gifts of fruits or pastries, or books that she might like. Marie stayed with Colleen's mother every week day while Colleen was at work during the school year. Colleen had previously had three home health aides who were not the right fit for her mother before Marie was assigned. Unlike the others, Marie was not indifferent, she was thoughtful; she was not a thief, she was dependable; and she did not complain about the amount of work it took to care for Colleen's mother, she was a true professional.

"Hello, Marie. How was she today?"

"Today was a challenge," Marie said.

"Why? What happened?" Marie had never given her such a negative report of the days' events, so this troubled Colleen.

"She refused to eat her lunch at first. She thought I was trying to poison her."

"Oh no," Colleen said.

"Then she went into the bathroom, turned on the faucet and locked the door."

"She does that with me a lot," Colleen admitted. "Did you use the key I gave you?"

"Yes. She didn't hurt herself. It seems she just wanted some time to herself. And also..." Here is where Marie hesitated. "She was saying cruel things about 'the girl who lives with' her. Really horrible and scary things. She was talking about *you*." There was compassion in Marie's voice and concern in the way she spoke.

Colleen sighed. She knew that there were times her mother didn't know her but there were also those occasions where her mother reacted to her with intense outbursts. Colleen quickly recalled the time her mother shoved her in an attempt to leave the apartment, claiming Colleen was keeping her prisoner.

"I'm not a child!" her mother had screamed in frustration. "You can't keep me locked up in this place!"

"You're right! And no, I don't want to treat you like a child. Why don't we go for a walk together?"

The mother had considered the suggestion and pouted her response. "We go where I want to go."

Colleen had agreed to her mother's demand, and the mother did not pull away when Colleen held her hand as they walked around the block.

"Well, I'll see you on Monday," Marie said, pulling Colleen back to the present.

"Thank you so much for your help with my mom today. And thank you for always being so patient with her."

Marie once again smiled with empathy. "Can I make a suggestion? For your safety and for your mother's, please consider finding her a permanent home. There's no telling what she might do to you or to herself." She gently touched Colleen's hands and said, "You deserve your own life."

Colleen thanked Marie one more time before seeing her out of the apartment. She quietly walked into her mother's bedroom to check in on her. The mother's eyes moved rapidly under the loose brown skin of her eyelids. Her deflated lips were pressed together in a pucker as she easily breathed through her nose. Despite the weathered hands that rested under her left cheek, the sleeping form of the mother paralleled that of an innocent child.

Colleen resembled the woman who raised her but knew that woman was long gone. In her place was a woman whose mannerisms was like that of an angry child who could not understand how to make sense of an unfamiliar world. Colleen knew and understood that as this woman's only child, she needed to take care of her and keep her safe. Not only was it what she and her dad had been planning on doing together before his heart attack, but it was also what her mother would have wanted, what she would have expected of Colleen.

She could still hear the words her mother told her and her dad when they learned of her diagnosis: "I feel so blessed knowing you both will be taking care of me. You have no idea what that means to me. I know whatever happens, I will be safe because of you."

No, there was no way Colleen could call the facility to inquire about full time care for her mother. She remembered the nights her mother sat by her bed with cold compresses when she was sick. The home-cooked meals, the sleepless nights during finals, the proud tears at her college graduation. How could she walk away from the person who gave her everything, even when she didn't recognize her anymore? With her father gone, Colleen knew the responsibility had to fall on her. The sleepless nights, the missed after-work events, and the stress of taking care of an ailing mother were all burdens she had gladly accepted as the only child to a woman who sacrificed the same for her as Colleen grew from a child to a young woman. Not only did Colleen feel her mother would have expected this of her, but she also felt it was her obligation.

Colleen wanted to get a head start for the following week and so spent her Friday evening working on lesson plans and grading her students' assignments. She could still hear Amber's voice suggesting that she do something fun just for her. Although lesson planning was the antithesis of fun, it was something just for her. Technically the lesson plan was for her students but the fact that it would diminish her anxiety on Monday morning after such a horrible day earlier, in Colleen's mind, deemed it an activity just for her.

The musical alarm on her phone suddenly ripped through the silence of the lonely living room. The time was 7pm. Colleen hated the idea of waking her mother up from her nap, but she needed to give her mother medication along with her dinner.

She slipped into her mother's room with a tray of food and set it on a small table by the bed, her movements soft and slow. She gently sat on the bed beside her sleeping mother.

"Hey, mom. It's time for your medication." Her voice was barely above a whisper.

She rested her hand on her mother's shoulder, careful not to alarm her. However, her calculated movements proved useless.

Her mother's eyes widened in terror. She took in a deep breath before sitting herself up on the bed. "No! Stay away from me!" the woman shrieked.

"Mom! It's just me!" Colleen tried to reassure her mother, tried to calm her down, to no avail. The woman kept screaming as she pushed herself away from Colleen in an attempt at a supposed escape. Wild-eyed, she looked all around her as if calculating her next move.

Colleen's voice was steady and controlled. "It's Colleen. Remember? I'm your daughter. Colleen."

"Leave me alone!"

In trying to get her mother to calm down, she reached for her and before she could comprehend what had happened, she felt a searing pain on her right cheekbone that traveled to the top of her head. She held that side of her face in her hand as she lifted herself from the bed. She regarded the mother in shock and saw that both of her mother's hands were balled into fists as she mouthed words Colleen could not hear. Her mother's fearful shouts were muffled by the agonizing sting that dominated all the physical and emotional feelings that now consumed Colleen. She pressed her hand to her cheek, stunned not just by the sting but by what it meant—her mother had struck her. The woman who once kissed her skinned knees and stayed up all night with her while she suffered with debilitating cramps attacked her.

A jumble of words raced through Colleen's mind.

I should be the one who cares for her, not a bunch of strangers.

"For your safety and for your mother's, please consider finding her a permanent home."

I can't just dump my mom in a nursing home.

"Give yourself some grace."

I need to take care of her and keep her safe. She would have wanted that.

The situation is not getting any easier.

"I feel so blessed to have you taking care of me. You have no idea what that means to me."

"You're being too hard on yourself."

Colleen trudged into the bathroom, still embracing the injured part of her face. She was taken aback by her bloodshot eyes displayed in the mirror. Examining her face, she confirmed there was no broken skin, but the right side of her face was quickly swelling up. In the kitchen, with trembling hands, she retrieved an ice pack from the freezer and softly placed it against her cheek, wincing from the pain. Back in the bathroom with the ice pack against her skin, she stared at her reflection as her mind continued racing with what had just transpired. Suddenly, aware of her mother's cries from the bedroom, Colleen realized that her mother had never stopped. Her mother was probably traumatized.

Seeming to temporarily forget the pain, Colleen rushed to her mother's room to find the woman still in her bed, swaying back and forth, sobbing. Cautiously, Colleen sat on the bed by her mother and tried to quiet her tears.

"Shh," she said, softly. "It's okay. It's all right."

She gently touched her mother's cheek with the palm of her hand, a gesture she remembered her father using in order to calm her mother down. Her mother's sobs reduced to a whimper as she closed her eyes and rested her head on her daughter's shoulder. Colleen let her head lean against her mother's and she wrapped her arms around her, holding her mother while humming *Amazing Grace*, the song she had heard Marie singing earlier that afternoon. Colleen held her mother until she felt her go limp in her arms, sleeping soundlessly.

Taking in a deep breath, Colleen gently lay her mother down on the bed and pulled a blanket over her. She kissed her mother on her forehead, took the tray of food and silently exited the room. After placing the food tray on the kitchen counter, Colleen walked back into the bathroom and once again placed the ice pack against her cheek. She stood in a daze, still reeling from what had just occurred.

Upon examining her face in the mirror, Colleen began to sense something deep within her that she was not expecting—a certain pride in herself.

Her smile was faint but it was there all the same.

"You're doing the best you can do," she told her reflection. "You love her and she knows it. You would never do anything to hurt her. You're a good daughter and you've always been. She needs more care than you can give her. You are doing the right thing by allowing professionals to care for her. You are a good daughter."

Legs heavy, she made her way into the living room, where her purse was. She reached into the side pocket and pulled out the business card for Gentle Hands Care Facility. She stared at the business card, her eyes stinging with tears. She thought about her father and worried whether he would have been disappointed in her. But why would he be? She wasn't giving up. She was instead giving both her mother and herself a chance to breathe again. Maybe giving herself grace didn't mean walking away—it meant not breaking down alongside the woman she still loved.

She had to believe that her father would have supported her decision. Amber was right; the way she was currently living was unhealthy and unsustainable. Not to mention, relieving the stress of being her mother's caretaker would help Colleen face work with a clearer mind. She would also be able to relax with friends in the evenings and on weekends. Her mother would be looked after by professionals who would know how to handle aggressive behavior. And of course she would visit her mother as often as possible. Yes, she thought. This was how she could care for her mother as well as showing herself some kindness. In the deepest part of her heart, this was what she knew her mother would have wanted for the both of them.

About Cathelina Duvert

Cathelina Duvert's debut novel, *The Box*, grew out of her own experiences with depression and earned an Honorable Mention in the 2024 Chapter One Writing Competition by Black Writers Workspace. In August 2025, she won First Place in the same contest for her forthcoming sophomore novel. Through her writing and speaking engagements, Duvert sheds light on mental health with honesty and heart. She lives in New York City with her twin sister and rescue kitten, Maxie. Learn more at www.cathelinaduvert.com

The Backup Plan

Heidi McIntyre

Brynn arrived early, as usual. The silence of the empty office spoke to her. It was exactly what she needed before the hustle—phones ringing, voices overlapping, and the nonstop rush of client urgency. She chose her favorite seat in the conference room, directly facing the wall of windows. With great care, she opened her laptop, placed her notepad next to it, and selected not one but two Sharpie pens, just in case.

From her perch on the 24th floor, Brynn watched the sun rise over Biscayne Bay. The sky lit up in shades of tangerine, fading to burnt orange at the horizon, which filled her with awe. This was why she'd moved to the Sunshine State. It was February in Miami, and there were no ice scrapers, snow shovels, or subzero temperatures in sight.

Brynn had been with Kent & Lockwood for over two years as an account executive. The consulting firm specialized in the food industry, representing both national brands and smaller startups that were constantly testing new products. Because of her passion for food, Brynn loved her job. But she was a shy, thoughtful introvert working in a fast-paced, extroverted environment. That was why these monthly staff meetings were especially jarring. Brynn hated the posturing for recognition, and how the team members rudely talked over each other.

"Good morning, Brynn," Daniela said, setting her laptop down at the head of the table. "I admire your dedication. First to arrive and last to leave."

Brynn blushed and nodded. Daniela's black hair was styled into a low bun. She looked confident in her leopard-print blouse and matching brown pants.

Just as Brynn was about to strike up a conversation, several more team members trickled in. Her mood shifted when she spotted James, a senior account executive, rushing over to whisper something to Daniela.

Her boss laughed, a high-pitched sound, and patted him on the back. Brynn's jaw tightened. James had a reputation for being "the closer." Other account executives whispered his name with reverence, marveling at his effortless ability to secure every deal.

But Brynn knew better. She was close friends with Jill, his assistant. James dedicated countless hours courting potential clients, while having Jill scour their social media to uncover all their interests and desires. If the contact was a Miami Dolphins fan, he'd provide tickets to the best sideline seats or club-level access.

Once James "bagged" the client, as he often bragged, he rarely looked at market research, preferring to rely on "a hunch." Jill was the one who developed the business and marketing plans, while James took all the credit.

"Let's get started," Daniela called out. "Everyone, please take a seat." She clicked the remote, dimming the lights as a large screen descended behind her. "I've got exciting news to share."

She clicked again, and a familiar brand logo appeared. "RootBerry is looking to expand into supermarkets. Their online store has been wildly successful since its 2020 launch. Last year alone, they made over two million in sales and..." She paused for emphasis. "They're looking for a consulting firm to assist with this new venture. We're on the list!"

Excitement stirred as Daniela reviewed the details on the screen. "RootBerry is a rising star in the health-conscious food market. They're known for their inventive line of sugar-free health bars made from unexpected, produce-forward ingredients like zucchini, kale, avocado, and citrus."

Brynn admired the company's mission. Founded by a nutritionist and a pastry chef, RootBerry was built on a loyal following of wellness-driven foodies, parents of picky eaters, and even diabetics craving guilt-free sweets. It was the perfect client.

Daniela continued, "They've grown organically through influencer partnerships, savvy social media, and positive press. Now the company is ready to scale up by selling directly to retailers, so they need help with the business strategy and marketing plan. That's where we come in."

"I'd like to get some initial ideas for the B2B strategy. This isn't a test," she emphasized. "There are no wrong answers. Don't be afraid to speak up."

Brynn cleared her throat, hands clenched under the table. She spoke in a low but steady voice. "They should start small. Test the waters by selling to health food stores and coffee shops. The intel they gain will help determine their pricing, merchandising, and—"

"That's one way to go," James interrupted. He leaned back in his chair, smirking like the cat who swallowed the cream.

Simmering with anger, Brynn kept her expression neutral while Jill gave her a sympathetic glance.

James continued, "I noticed the words 'Keto Free' printed in tiny letters on the packaging. Keto isn't a fad anymore. I suggest updating the design and creating a merchandising display with 'KETO FREE' in bold on the header. Retailers cater to millennial shoppers because of the immense size of this demographic."

Daniela smiled. "Interesting. Any other ideas?" The silence was awkward since no one dared to cross the boss's pet. After a full minute, she smiled politely, but Brynn noticed Daniela's fingers tapping anxiously against the table.

"James, I'd like you to take the lead on developing the proposal, but..." She paused for emphasis. "...please include Brynn as part of your team."

The tension dissolved as the group eagerly nodded. Brynn rolled her eyes, deflated.

The good news was her boss must've been concerned about James's pitch, or she wouldn't have added her to his team, but Brynn doubted James would take her ideas seriously. RootBerry was asking for a business plan, not an ad campaign with a merchandising gimmick.

Founder Steve Ames had strategically managed the company's rise. Her idea of targeting smaller stores as a first step would've allowed RootBerry to test and refine their inventory planning, pricing and merchandising before scaling up. The results could attract larger retailers like Starbucks and Whole Foods.

After the meeting ended and Daniela left the room, Brynn watched James bask in the admiration of the junior staffers.

It didn't matter how smart or prepared she was. With James' oversized ego and charm, she would always be invisible.

As tears threatened, Brynn felt the urge to escape. She packed her laptop, notepad then headed out the door. Her favorite coffee shop was just a few blocks away.

She reached the lobby as the elevator doors opened. Perfect timing. She didn't want the group to see her leave. Brynn hurried inside and pressed the button for the first floor.

As the doors closed, a strangled cry escaped. Tears rolled down her cheeks. When the elevator reached the twentieth floor, it stopped. She waited. Nothing. The lights flickered. A jolt startled her, but then nothing.

She held her breath, counting the seconds. The elevator didn't move. Frustration boiled up from within. Brynn slammed her fist against the steel wall and winced, but it felt good to release her pent-up rage.

"It can't be all that bad?" A male voice said behind her.

Brynn froze. In her rush, she hadn't noticed a man in the opposite corner. Mortified, she pulled a tissue from her backpack and dabbed her eyes.

"Sorry, I thought I was alone."

"No problem. Hey, are you okay?"

"Yep. Just having a bad day."

"Did you get fired?"

She didn't recognize his voice, so luckily it wasn't someone from the firm. "Nope. A narcissistic idiot cut me off before I could present my idea. His dumb plan was chosen."

"Does that happen a lot?"

"Yep. Hey, the elevator's still stuck. Should we call someone?"

He stepped forward and pressed the open-door button.

She peeked at him. He was attractive—a cream-colored shirt soft enough to sleep in, dark jeans, and worn-in leather boots. Not the typical executive type.

He pushed the button again. Nothing.

When he turned, she was struck by his amber eyes. They were magnetic.

"I'm going to hit the emergency button. It'll be loud." He cautioned.

She nodded.

His finger hovered, then pressed. The alarm rang, followed by a beep, then static. Finally, a man's voice crackled through.

"Service desk. Can you hear me?"

"Yes, we're stuck on the twentieth floor. Two of us," the guy said.

"Understood. You're safe. Maintenance is on the way."

"Thanks."

He ran his fingers through his thick hair, tousling it. A shadow of stubble softened his jaw. He looked to be around her age, twenty-eight.

"Looks like we'll be here a while. I'm Brynn."

He grinned and held out his hand. "Levi."

His grip was warm and solid. Brynn didn't let go right away. She blushed.

"Do you work in the building?" She asked, trying to pivot from that awkward moment.

"Kind of. I'm a creative director at Latitude 25. I come in on Mondays. The rest of the week, I work from home."

She was familiar with the advertising agency. They'd just moved into the building a few months ago. "Wow, they let you work remotely?"

"Helps that I'm a partner."

"Really? What made you decide to start your own business?"

He looked amused. "Good question. Most people want to know what it's *like* to work at an ad agency. I worked sixty-hour weeks at my previous job. Every decision had to be approved by a committee. The account execs never understood my point of view. My work got so watered down that by the time it reached the client, it was a shell of what it could've been."

"A buddy of mine was the VP of client services. He got some angel investors and asked me to join him in the startup. I jumped, and we never looked back."

"Why did you move to this building?"

"We needed more room to grow since we're adding a market research division. But enough about me. What do you do? Tell me about the idiot who's stealing your thunder."

Brynn sighed. "I'm an account exec at Kent & Lockwood. James pitches mediocre ideas. But he's known as the closer, so everyone thinks he walks on water."

"Ah, I know the type. Who was the client?"

"RootBerry. I love their mission. Super-healthy, delicious products. They donate a portion of sales to food banks."

Levi's eyebrows furrowed. He leaned back against the elevator wall. "The mango-nut bar is my favorite. The avocado ingredient makes it extra creamy." His voice dimmed, which was odd.

"Good choice," she said. "My favorite is the berry-dream bar. I've got a serious sweet tooth."

Levi nodded. "Hey... since we're stuck, I'm curious about your pitch."

"Really, why?"

"Why not? We've got time to kill, and I'm a good listener. Maybe I can give you some tips."

Brynn blinked, surprised. "This is confidential, right?"

"Your secret is safe with me."

She shared her thoughts, including what James had proposed. He listened intently, then frowned. "Your idea is both smart and strategic. James' pitch sounds more like ad fluff, not an actual business plan."

"That's what I thought!"

"You shouldn't let him silence you."

"You're right. I've been with the firm for two years, but I still feel like a newbie. The staff meetings are intimidating."

"Do you want revenge? Put James in his place?"

She smiled. "You bet, but that will never happen."

"What if the client hates his pitch? You should be ready to step in and present your idea."

"Daniela, my boss, would be furious. I'd get fired."

"Not if the client loves your ideas." He paused. "I bet they will."

"You really think so?"

"Absolutely. Hey, I can help you with the presentation. I'll use my graphic skills to jazz it up, make it even more impressive."

"No, I couldn't ask you to do that."

"You didn't. I offered." She tilted her head, studying him.

Was he just being kind, or was there something more behind his offer? Either way, it didn't matter. No one had taken her ideas seriously in a long time, let alone noticed *her*. She felt an unfamiliar flutter in her belly.

Levi spoke up. "Listen, I've been where you are, so I know how you feel. What should we call it?"

Her eyes lit up. "The Backup Plan."

"Perfect."

The elevator jolted, then moved smoothly downward. When it opened on the first floor, Levi handed her his card.

"Call or text when you're ready."

"Thank you. This day is turning out better than I expected."

He grinned and walked away.

It had been over a week since the elevator incident. Brynn wasn't looking forward to attending James's brainstorming session, especially since he rarely took her advice.

Because it was a small conference room, she couldn't sit apart from the group. James was already there with his two wide-eyed junior account execs. She took a deep breath, determined to be a team player.

"Let's get started." James launched into a detailed explanation of the benefits of his keto campaign. When he finished, Brynn tried her best not to roll her eyes.

"That's an interesting concept." She kept her tone diplomatic. "I agree that keto is popular and not just a diet trend, but my concern is we're not addressing the larger business strategy RootBerry requested in their proposal. Why don't we combine..."

"What the hell, Brynn." James interrupted. "Why do you always have to be a buzz killer? You know what your problem is?" He didn't wait for an answer. "You lack vision."

Brynn gritted her teeth as James launched into a twenty-minute tirade about his "winning strategy." It sucked the air out of the room.

When she returned to her office, she blew out a breath of frustration before remembering Levi's card. It remained tucked inside the front pocket of her purse. Brynn pulled it out and read the details: Levi Adler, Managing Partner & Creative Director, Latitude 25.

She thought about his enthusiasm. *I'd love to see your idea.* What if he was just being polite? It didn't matter. That bizarre meeting with James was the last straw. She held her breath, grabbed her personal cell phone, and texted Levi.

> **Brynn:** *Hey, it's Brynn from the elevator. Still want to hear my idea?*

She figured it would take a day or two for him to respond, if at all. Five minutes later, her cell pinged.

> **Levi:** *You bet. Mornings work better for me. Let's meet at a coffee shop. How about this Friday, 6:30 am? You pick the place.*

> **Brynn:** *Sounds good. I'll meet you at Manam on 26th St. Thanks!*

> **Levi:** *Good choice! See you then.*

She was adding it to her calendar when a voice rang out from behind.

"Good morning." With a jolt, Brynn put her phone down. When she saw it was Jill, relief flooded her veins.

"You're jumpy this morning?"

"Must've been that double espresso," Brynn quipped. "I didn't sleep well last night."

"No wonder after that brainstorming session yesterday. James keeps bringing it up. He acts self-assured, but deep down, he's insecure. Whatever you said, it bothered him."

"Yeah, well, the truth hurts. I said it nicely, but I can't pretend his plan is good."

"I agree. He wants me to do some..." Jill air-quoted. "'Deep-dive research' into the evolution of the keto trend. Sounds lame to me."

"I don't get why Daniela supports this idea?"

"She's not fully on board, which is why she pressed him to make sure you were on his team. My guess is she was hoping the two of you could hash it out."

"Not happening."

"Do want me to talk to him, smooth things over?"

"I appreciate your willingness to help, but we're never going to agree."

"Okay, but if there's anything I can do, let me know."

Manam was Brynn's favorite cafe. Close to the office, it was famous for its lush, Miami-inspired floral displays, which exuded a cozy indoor-outdoor atmosphere. She arrived early so she could get settled in, open her laptop, and take a few deep breaths to calm her nerves.

The cafe was quieter than she expected, with the soft hum of conversation, the hiss of the espresso machine, and indie folk music playing in the background. Brynn scanned the room for a quiet corner when those amber eyes met hers. She gasped.

Levi sat near the window with the same easy smile she remembered from the elevator. He dressed casually, a navy button-down with sleeves rolled and a knit beanie shoved halfway into his jacket pocket. Something about him radiated warmth, like he belonged in this place.

"You beat me," she blurted, her voice a notch too high. "I thought I was chronically early."

He laughed, pushing his iced coffee aside. "I woke up earlier than usual. Plus, it's a cool place to hang out."

Brynn put her backpack on the table. "I come here when I need to get away from the office. In fact, I was headed here when we got stuck in the elevator."

"At least we won't need an escape hatch here," he joked.

Brynn smiled despite herself. "I've already plotted at least three exits. I may be quiet, but I'm highly strategic."

Levi's eyes widened in mock admiration. "Didn't peg you as a survivalist."

"You'd be surprised. Working at a consulting firm with junior execs clamoring for my job, I've learned to be prepared for every outcome." She grinned, the tension easing from her chest.

"That's why we're here." Levi declared.

The server came and went. Brynn ordered a honey-lavender latte, trying to remember if her voice sounded normal. Levi made small talk about the cafe, how he used to come here when deadlines piled up. She nodded along, clutching the mug when it arrived, letting the heat settle into her fingers.

He was so at ease it amazed her. The way he looked directly at her when she spoke, not through her — like he was actually listening.

"I'm eager to see your idea." Levi leaned forward.

Brynn pulled out her tablet and notepad from her bag. She gave him a quick overview before nervously sliding her tablet across the table. "This is the first draft. Nothing fancy yet."

Levi smiled. "My previous agency once pitched a yogurt brand with hand puppets. I'm pretty open-minded."

He tapped through the deck slowly, nodding, occasionally murmuring "hmm" and "Interesting."

Brynn twisted her ring. "You can be honest. I can take it."

Levi set the tablet down. "I think it's smart. Especially the way you linked RootBerry's mission to emotional nourishment. It's not just about healthy food; it's about belonging."

"That's exactly what I was trying to say." A flicker of confidence took root in her chest.

Levi quirked an eyebrow. "I'm curious. How do you define belonging?"

"Their products are not only for the health-conscious consumer, but for those with dietary restrictions too, which is why they use their social media to educate consumers. Plus, they give a percentage of every product sold to charity. RootBerry has built an inclusive, loyal following by serving a need while also solving a problem."

He leaned forward. "Then say it louder. Let's make this your through-line."

Brynn's smile caught her by surprise. "Good point. What do you suggest?"

"We'll come up with a tagline to add to the presentation's template design. Then I'll use graphics to amplify the message with a short video intro."

"You make it sound so easy."

"The graphics are easy for me, unlike the concept, which is more challenging. Luckily, yours is solid and original. That makes it more fun to design."

His words were like an exhale she hadn't realized she'd been holding. For the first time in days, she felt free, and unchained.

The screen flickered to life. As she sat at her kitchen table, Brynn adjusted the laptop angle while she waited for Levi to join her on Zoom. Since their coffee shop meeting a week ago, she was pleased with the latest results. When she looked up, Levi was waiting to be admitted.

He sipped from a ceramic mug that read: *I Do My Own Stunts.* Levi raised an eyebrow. "Wow. Your kitchen is...very white."

Brynn glanced behind her. "The plant on the windowsill is green."

"No judgment," he said, grinning. "Is it always that spotless?"

She laughed, surprised by how easy it felt. "Let's see yours."

"Hell no. You'd run for the hills," he groaned.

They got to work. Brynn shared the presentation deck and walked him through the revised strategy. Levi offered light edits that were mostly encouraging. They scheduled their next session.

She closed the deck. "You've got good instincts," he asserted. "I like to see you trust them more."

"You're right. I often find myself second-guessing decisions which is why I don't speak up as much as I should. I wasn't like that at my last job. This company can be unnerving."

He leaned closer to the screen. "Think of this as a test. Stepping outside your comfort zone is the best way to build courage."

"Thanks Levi. I really like what we're creating. It's been a while since I've had this much fun working."

The following week, Brynn was ready for their next Zoom meeting at 8:30 pm. She'd donned a soft peach sweater and styled her light-brown hair instead of wearing it in a ponytail before applying lip gloss and mascara. Brynn wanted to look more professional — at least that's what she told herself.

Levi was lounging on a sofa this time, sketchpad in hand. He wore a fitted T-shirt, which accentuated his muscular arms and chest. Her pulse raced.

"I've been noodling with the tagline," he said. "Yours is close, but something's missing."

Brynn exhaled. "I had one I liked better, but it felt... edgy."

He cocked an eyebrow. "Hit me with it."

She clicked through to a hidden draft slide. *Bite. Boost. Better the World.*

Levi whooped. "You nailed it. It's bold yet relatable."

"You think they'll like it?"

"Honestly? They'd be crazy not to. Either way, you'll get their attention."

For the first time, Brynn felt like her ideas had weight.

The next day, Brynn headed to the break room to grab a snack when she spotted Jill sitting at the table, coffee cup in hand. "Hey, can you sit for a minute?"

"Sure." Brynn grabbed a banana and sat next to her.

Jill whispered. "Everyone's chattering about the staff meeting yesterday. How you corrected James when he presented the research data on RootBerry. I'm bummed I was at a doctor's appointment. I'd give anything to see the look on his face."

Brynn smiled. "Yeah, he looked shocked, and lost his train of thought, but he didn't seem mad about it."

"That's because Daniela was there. He won't lose his cool in front of her. I'm more surprised you stood up to him. You're typically quiet at those meetings."

"That's the problem. It's time I became more assertive."

"Good for you. Someone needs to put James in his place."

Brynn arrived at Levi's apartment on Saturday morning. As she rode up the elevator to the top floor, she felt jittery. It was much more intimate meeting at his place, especially since she was having feelings for her mentor. For all she knew, he could be married or have a girlfriend.

Located in the Wynwood Arts District, his building had an artsy, industrial vibe. She rang the doorbell.

"It's open. Come on in." Levi called out.

The size of his loft-style apartment impressed Brynn. Exposed brick walls featured shelves that displayed design books and quirky art. She recognized the black-leather sectional couch and followed Levi's voice into the kitchen.

He was whisking a mixture in a large steel bowl. The counter was a mess, filled with pieces of onions, avocado skins plus diced tomato strewn across the surface.

"Can I get you a coffee or iced tea?"

"No, thanks. You're cooking?"

"More like assembling. It's guacamole. I figured we'd have a snack before lunch." He picked up the bowl and his drink tumbler. "Can you grab the chips?" Brynn's hand twitched with the urge to grab a sponge and tackle the mess. Instead, she picked up the bag and followed him up the stairs.

Levi's office was sleek, and modern with hardwood floors, framed artwork and built-in bookcases. She spotted a small couch facing his desk, sat down, and pulled out her notepad. Brynn had already sent the presentation to Levi a few days ago, so she was eager to see his design skills.

He turned his large screen to face her. "Check out this opening."

The images of a family enjoying a snack, a woman jogging on a trail, and a boy at soccer practice were on point. Folk music played in the background. The effect was warm and uplifting, ending with Bite. Boost. Better the World in bold letters.

"Wow, it's so much better than what I'd envisioned," she exclaimed, clapping her hands.

"It's the voice they need to hear. Confident like you." The heat in his gaze was electric.

Brynn blushed but didn't look away. "It's us, actually."

Levi smiled. "Here's the page design." He tapped the slide to showcase a colorful layout that matched RootBerry's brand image.

"Looks amazing. Now we can add the content. I completed the outline based on my notes from our last meeting."

They worked side-by-side for the next two hours, pausing only for takeout and conversation. Between drafts, they shared stories. Levi described the horrible pitch (hand puppets again), and Brynn told him more about what it was like to work at Kent & Lockwood. She confessed her fear of being "not enough," how exhausting it felt to work in such a competitive, cutthroat environment.

He didn't rush to reassure her. Just listened. Then said, "I know exactly what you're going through."

Levi saved the presentation into a folder labeled "Just in case" and handed her the thumb drive.

"If the client likes Jame's idea, they'll never get to see this. That thought keeps me up at night," she whispered.

"What matters is you've got the brains and talent to turn an idea into a dynamic business plan. Your work speaks louder than his swagger ever could."

Brynn felt gratitude toward Levi and the plan they'd created, not because she knew she'd present it, but because for once she felt proud of her voice.

Her eyes dotted with tears. "Do you really think so?"

He moved to sit down next to her. "You bet I do. The hard work is done. The only thing left is to breathe." He gently touched her wrist.

"You always know what to say." Their eyes met. The moment lingered, charged with a silent understanding.

Two days later, the air in the conference room was heavy, scented faintly with coffee and anticipation. Brynn sat two seats down from James, notebook on the table, hands folded tightly in her lap to keep them from shaking. She glanced over at Jill, who sat next to James. Her friend looked bored and maybe a little embarrassed, since they both knew what James was presenting.

Daniela stood at the head of the table and greeted the RootBerry team as they entered, including Steve Ames, the CEO she'd long admired. "James will walk us through our proposed strategy," she announced.

James clicked the remote. A bold slide appeared: "KETO FREE = FREEDOM," accompanied by images of trendy grocery shelves and influencer-style photos.

His voice was a little too upbeat. "Today's consumers want both healthy and flavorful solutions. Keto-free isn't just a label. It's a lifestyle. Gen Z and Millennials both exhibit a desire for freedom and a willingness to challenge norms." He spent the next twenty minutes reviewing endless research charts to back up his point before moving on.

"We suggest a national rollout that plays on the theme of rebellion and freedom. Think: 'Dessert Without Chains.'"

Brynn bit back the urge to laugh. She glanced at the RootBerry founder, Steve Ames. His brow furrowed. The other team members exchanged startled glances.

James was oblivious, but Daniela's lips pursed, like she'd swallowed a lemon. He pressed on. "We'll use aggressive color, minimal text, and imaginative social media, videos with athletes, skateboarders, and perhaps even a TikTok dance challenge."

Brynn's stomach twisted. Skateboarders?!

A very long pause followed the last slide. Then Steve spoke, polite but blunt. "Thank you, James. I appreciate the energy, but this doesn't really align with our mission. We're not here to chase trends. We're about nourishment, inclusion, and flavorful products."

"I'm also confused because our proposal explicitly asked for a strategic business plan with a marketing strategy. We're not looking for another advertising agency."

Daniela nodded, trying to recover. "I understand. What if we change..."

"Actually, there is." Brynn stood up, voice low but steady.

As the room turned to face her, she blinked, heart pounding in her ears. "There's another concept we've been working on. I'd love to show it to you."

Daniela's eyes widened, but she didn't object. Brynn walked to the screen. While she was plugging in her tablet, her boss whispered. "I hope you know what you're doing."

Levi's intro video looked even better on the large screen. It ended with the first slide showing RootBerry's logo with the tagline: *Bite. Boost. Better the World.*

Brynn cleared her throat. "We believe RootBerry's strength is in its authenticity. You're selling sincerity. Whether it's parents of kids with dietary restrictions, or wellness-conscious consumers who want more flavor with less sugar, or that high-school graduate who can now go to college thanks to your scholarship program. Your brand is indulgence with purpose."

Slide by slide, she walked them through each section: A phased rollout in key urban markets, the focus on strategic partnerships with cafes and smaller grocers as their testing ground, ideas for several themed merchandising displays, and messaging tied to emotional nourishment and social service.

Then the tagline that made Levi grin when she'd first said it: *Bite. Boost. Better the World.*

She ended with a soft smile. "RootBerry isn't about fitting in. It's about being remembered for the right reasons."

The room was silent, but Brynn stood firm. Finally, she'd stood up for herself. Whatever the consequences, she'd never regret this moment.

Then Steve leaned back, lips curved in a slow smile. "Now that's more like it."

James looked deflated. Brynn let out the breath she'd been holding. The mood lightened as heads nodded while Daniela beamed.

Then Steve added, "We'd love to bring in our agency to build off this. We're working with Latitude 25 on our brand image and identity."

Wait, what? Brynn's eyes grew wide.

"Of course," Daniela replied. "We'll be happy to coordinate with them, especially since we're both in the same building. Any more questions?"

Brynn stood still, lips pressed tight. The warmth she'd felt moments ago had curdled into disbelief. She trusted this guy, shared way too much information, and now he'd betrayed her? It made little sense.

Steve continued. "Brynn, I'm impressed with your thoughtful presentation. You obviously did your homework."

"Thank you, Steve. I admire how you've been able to grow RootBerry so quickly. Of course, it helps that your products are so delicious."

Daniela chimed in. "Yes, Brynn has only been with us for two years, but she's created quite a stir."

"If you can provide me with the budget breakdown as outlined in the proposal, we'll then forward the contract." Steve declared.

"Brynn will send that to you before the end of the week." Daniela clapped her hands. "Well! We're thrilled to support your new endeavor."

An hour later, Brynn sat at her desk staring at the Excel file with RootBerry's budget broken down into sections as the proposal had requested. She pretended to be deep in thought, but inside she was unraveling.

"Hey there."

She turned to see Levi holding a bouquet.

"I don't get it. Why didn't you tell me?"

"I didn't know RootBerry had sent your company a proposal. When we met in the elevator, it piqued my curiosity. I should've been upfront with you after you shared your ideas, but I knew the client would love your proposal. I just wanted to give it a chance to be seen."

He placed the flowers on her desk. "I was wrong for not telling you sooner. I'm sorry."

She crossed her arms over her chest. "I trusted you, told you all those things about my job and the firm."

"Please believe me. I will never breathe a word to anyone."

"Says the guy who lied."

"Brynn, I'd planned to tell you… I really did. It wasn't just the pitch I cared about. It was you. As we got to know each other, my feelings grew deeper, so I kept putting it off. Then it was too late."

She pointed to the door. "I've got to finish this budget. Please go." Brynn turned back to her screen.

"I hope you can forgive me." Levi said and walked away.

A few minutes later, she heard footsteps approaching. "What now?" She exclaimed, frustrated.

"Whoa, what's gotten into you?" Daniela chided. "I figured you'd be celebrating."

The blood drained from Brynn's face. "I'm so sorry. I thought you were someone else."

Daniela sat in the chair facing her desk. "Was it James? I know he's disappointed. He's not taking it out on you, is he?"

"No, it's nothing. I'm fine."

"Thank you for saving the pitch. I'm kicking myself for not overseeing this process more closely. I made the mistake of trusting James when he promised me he'd include your ideas. That won't happen again."

She leaned forward. "When you stood up, I didn't know what to think. Yet, you commanded the room like a pro. Your presentation was smart and on point. I'll make sure you get a hefty bonus for your hard work."

"Thank you, Daniela. This means a lot to me."

After she left. Levi's words kept spinning in her head. Brynn needed advice fast. She rushed over to Jill's desk and pointed towards the elevator. Her friend nodded, and they both headed to the lobby. By the time the elevator door opened, Jill was right behind.

"You rocked that presentation! James is spitting nails. Daniela told him you were the MVP on this project. I'm so proud of you."

"Thanks." Brynn's voice cracked as a tear ran down her cheek.

"Oh, no. James didn't upset you, did he?"

Brynn nodded her head no as the tears fell. The elevator door opened on the lobby level. Jill took her arm and led her out the door. They walked in silence until they reached Biscayne Bay. Being near the ocean calmed Brynn's nerves.

Jill put her arm around her shoulder. "What happened?"

"I met this guy in the elevator," she stammered, then described all that had occurred between her and Levi.

Jill tilted her head. "And that's a problem?"

"He's a partner and creative director at Latitude 25. I didn't know RootBerry was their client."

"Oh boy, that sucks. He should've told you upfront, but it's not like he stole your idea. Did you ask him why?"

"He stopped by my office." Brynn repeated what Levi had said.

"Is he hot?"

"Really? He betrayed me."

"Sort of, but maybe not. He's guilty of omission, for sure. If he had wanted to betray you, he would've presented your idea to the client as his own. Instead, he helped you make it better, more impactful. It sounds to me like he wanted you to win." She paused. "How old is he?"

Brynn rolled her eyes. "Thirty, and yes, he's hot."

"I knew it! Sounds like his feelings for you impeded what started out as a win-win collaboration. In the end, he was afraid of losing you."

Brynn blew out a long breath. "Maybe I judged him too harshly."

"I get it. He should've said something way before the presentation. It was a shock. Yet, since the two of you have been working together, you've changed in a good way."

"You're more assertive at meetings, more willing to share your ideas. It's like you've come out of your shell. Then you knocked that presentation out of the park. I saw the stunned look on Daniela's face. I'd think twice about this guy if I were you."

The scent of vanilla filled the air as Brynn approached Levi's apartment. She held a worn ceramic pie dish wrapped in a tea towel–her favorite homemade custard tart. It was the same recipe her grandmother used when Brynn was having a rough time in middle school. It tasted sweet and not at all fancy, but it was hers.

When Levi opened the door, he looked surprised. "Hey."

She held out the dish. "Peace offering. I brought you something sweet, an old family recipe."

He stepped back to let her in, eyes softening. "You didn't have to—"

"I wanted to."

They stood in the kitchen. Sadness lingered in the air. Levi ran a hand through his hair. "I screwed up. I should've told you about RootBerry the second I found out." He paused, gathering his thoughts. "I didn't want to ruin whatever was happening between us."

Brynn set the dish down on the counter. "I get it now. You weren't trying to deceive me. You believed in my idea and wanted the client to see it."

He looked at her earnestly. "I didn't just believe in your pitch. I believed in you."

Brynn felt his words settle in her chest. "I know. It has meant the world to me." She smiled, eyes glinting. "I just had to believe in me first."

Levi grinned, half-relieved. "So, we're friends again?"

She stepped closer. "I don't think so. You see, friends don't kiss."

His brows lifted. "No?"

She leaned in while he met her halfway. The kiss was gentle, slow, filled with promise.

For once, Brynn didn't just have a seat at the table. She'd found her voice. And it tasted like home.

About Heidi McIntyre

Always an avid reader, Heidi was inspired to write by her college professor who convinced her to switch majors to English. From then on, she harbored a secret wish to write a novel.

She spent most of her marketing career as a consultant specializing in fresh produce where she worked with a variety of growers, commodity boards, and associations. Her marketing campaigns received multiple awards.

Sea Magic is her debut novel and the first of the Hidden Gems series, which was also a finalist in the 2022 Page Turner Awards. Her second novel in the series, *Dark River Magic*, will launch in the Spring of 2026. Heidi lives in Oviedo, Florida with her husband, Tim, and their dogs Pumpkin and Lizzie. She loves coffee, chocolate, yoga, and visiting historical places.

For more information about Heidi and updates, go to: https://heidimcintyre.com/

World World

JANET KOOPS

Tammy opened her eyes, seeing nothing but the mountain of boxes pinning her to the floor as if she were the bottom piece of a collapsed Jenga tower.

Dare she move? Could she move?

She wiggled her fingers and then her toes. Nothing appeared to be broken, but she'd definitely have some bruises tomorrow. If Hal, her ex-husband, could see her now, he'd be giving her an "I told you so" with a simple shake of his head. But he'd help her up, regardless. Hal was that kind of guy. If only she had her phone.

Love hurt; life had taught her that. But this? To be hurt by her deepest, purest love? This surprised her.

The origins of her love could be traced back to grade seven. A boy had sat behind her in math class, and one day he reached forward and snapped her bra strap. She let out a yelp, turning to face a smug David Pepperman. It was the first day she'd ever worn one, and it was back when a girl still felt self-conscious about anyone seeing her underwear.

The class laughed, and deep in her humiliation, something else snapped, too. Tammy let go of a string of vicious words unlike any she'd said before, and they had only one target: David Pepperman's lower anatomy.

The boys erupted in more laughter. The girls gazed at her in admiration. David's face blossomed into a patchy tomato red.

At the same time, Tammy's entire body flooded with something new, something different: power.

Of course, a shocked Mrs. Findlay, the math teacher, sent Tammy to the principal's office—another first. She received a two-day suspension and, later that night, a two-week grounding from her parents. But these events did nothing to diminish her power.

The power of words.

On her return to school, she sought out David Pepperman to thank him for changing her life, but he avoided her.

She attempted to catch him at the end of the day, and as the hot June sun shone down on the schoolyard, she shaded her eyes and watched as David Pepperman ran full speed across the field then down a street toward his house. Tammy couldn't believe it. She'd caused that with nothing more than words. As David got smaller and smaller, her love of words grew.

On her way home that day, Tammy stopped by the corner store and spent her babysitting allowance on a journal and new pen. She can still remember the crack of the spine, the smell of the new pages, and the smooth texture of the paper as she ran her finger along crisp blue lines. Her pen revealed more magic. Words in delicate blue ink bloomed across the page as she wrote, so words were not only powerful, they were beautiful, too.

Of course, Tammy learned calligraphy. She became so good she earned money in college by creating logos and filling out certificates. In fact, she designed her and Hal's wedding invitation. Her husband had admired her handiwork then. He'd also liked that, as a freelance writer, Tammy worked from home–dinner was always waiting for him after work. What he hadn't liked was her dedication.

Not that Tammy could blame him. She was truly happy only while writing. Still was. For thirty years, she'd surrounded herself with words. Literally. Tammy saved everything she wrote, from grocery lists to every draft of an article, to the manuscript that grew and grew because she dare not edit or delete one single word.

Hal had insisted she switch to a computer, the silly man thinking she'd save everything to the hard drive. She did, of course, but she continued printing everything, too.

It took a while for her collection to build. Once the bookcases were full, piles began to form, then the piles became stacks, and those stacks became boxes. Words filled her house, floor to ceiling, but Tammy didn't mind. They gave her life and in return, she gave hers. Isn't that what you do for true love?

And speaking of love, late at night, among her boxes, that's what Tammy dreamed of. Beautiful love in sweet, delicate fonts. She loved that about the computer: access to so many fonts. Some were refined and elegant with a touch of romance, like a love letter from Paris. If she wanted a giggle, she'd choose a silly font, one with loops and curls. The chaos of it never failed to make her laugh.

When was the last time she laughed?

Not recently. Not since the ugly words began falling through her mail slot. *Condemned. Unsafe. Unfit for habitation.* They reminded her of years ago, of equally nasty words. *Divorce. Custody. Unstable.*

Stacked up to the ceiling, Tammy believed her words kept her safe. But the town's bylaw officers had a different opinion.

One letter had arrived that morning, and Tammy panicked. To prevent any more filth from penetrating her mail slot and contaminating her house, she moved some of her boxes, stacking them against the front door. Repositioning these boxes revealed fuzzy black markings on the wall, like furry ink spots. Tammy touched them ever so gently. They were soft and damp. *Organic words*, she thought, *living words, oh my.*

They were still babies, growing so slowly the words were unrecognizable. But soon they would be clear and larger than life! Someone, no, not someone, *something*, some greater power, was writing on her walls. Her world was merging with the words she loved, and it filled her heart with joy.

Not just any old joy—she ran to her computer, searching for something more whimsical and light-hearted. JOY. JOY. JOY. She typed it over and over again, in different sizes and different fonts, filling an entire page.

Tammy sent it to the printer.

Hearing the materialization of her joy overwhelmed her, and she threw herself against her boxes. Wondering. Marveling.

And that's when the trouble began. Tammy didn't realize how strong her enthusiasm was. Around her, boxes began shaking, and as she lay there, euphoric, it began raining words.

Just a few at first, and then there was a tremor. After that, they came fast and furious. Words emanated from all corners, of all sizes and shapes. They were louder than expected, heavier, too, but she opened herself up and surrendered to the weight of them all.

And that's how she found herself trapped on the floor. She could barely move, and the weight on her chest made breathing difficult.

Was this how she went? Death by words?

The pen was indeed mightier than the sword.

I'm not ready. Not yet. Tammy didn't have many regrets, but everyone has a few. Her relationship with her daughter was her biggie. They hadn't spoken in years, and Tammy longed to heal all that was broken.

The last time Tammy had reached out, Parola (literally, Italian for *word*) refused to meet unless Tammy cleaned the house. Why couldn't the girl understand how important the words were? How beautiful?

That was over five years ago. She didn't want to die without Parola knowing that she was the only thing Tammy valued more than words.

But stuck under all those boxes with nothing to do but think, Tammy wondered if that was true. She'd not argued when the court assigned Hal full custody. She'd not fought, nor made any attempt to tidy the house.

Of course she knew her organic words were black mold. Her house was a death trap, but the illusion of love and safety in her words was too strong to walk away from. How she preferred it to the ache of loneliness and the mess her life had become.

Perhaps she deserved to die like this.

"Oh, nonsense." Her mother's voice boomed so loud it was hard to believe it came from her own mind. "Just do it, girl."

How many times had her mother said that? Too many to count, but her mother was usually right, and today was no different. If only her mother were there. Tammy would do anything for one more reassuring hug, wrapped in her mother's warm arms and the scent of roses. Her mother had never let her down. *Just do it.*

"Okay, okay," Tammy said aloud. If she was going to survive, she'd have to crawl her way out. No, Tammy didn't like the shape of that word. *Crawl* didn't convey her reality. There wasn't enough room for her to get on her hands and knees. *Slither, squirm, wriggle.* Yes, those were better.

So that's what Tammy did, inch by painstaking inch, somehow dragging herself to safety through the scattered, and occasionally sharp, debris of her life.

When she finally reached the back door, perspiration trickled down her face, and her arms ached. She practically slid down the stairs, inhaling deeply the scent of a distant lilac bush.

Exhausted, she reached her beloved maple tree and collapsed against its trunk. Her lungs hurt, and she coughed. The bark was rough against her back, but she didn't care.

Overwhelmed with life, fear, existential dread, and everything else she could think of, she began to cry, loud gut-wrenching sobs that shook her entire body.

"Can I help?" The voice startled her.

Tammy glanced around, wiping at her face, as she attempted to stop crying. She saw no one.

"Up here," the voice said. Friendly. Confident. Young. If it were a font, it would be Antic. Perhaps Roboto.

Unlike her mother's voice, this one belonged to a real person.

A young woman with big brown eyes and short blond hair peered over the fence, fingers holding onto the wooden boards. "Are you okay?"

"Yes. Fine. Thanks." Tammy replied.

"Are you sure? Because you're bleeding. I'm training to become a paramedic, so hang on, I'll be right over with my kit."

The woman disappeared from view before Tammy could protest.

Moments later, Tammy's side gate creaked open and the young woman entered the backyard, wading through grass up to her knees.

"I'm Alice," she said. "Were you in an accident?"

Tammy attempted a smile. They hadn't met before because Tammy rarely went outside, and all the neighbors avoided her. "I'm Tammy. I fell. Then something fell on me."

"Wow. Well, I'm just going to give you a quick exam, make sure you don't have a head injury, and then clean your knee. You seem to have cut it pretty badly. Your arm's a bit scraped up, too."

Instead of retreating into her house, Tammy remained there, nodding in agreement. She'd run out of steam, as depleted and empty as an expended ink cartridge.

Alice opened her first-aid kit, put on gloves, and began the examination. The girl (she couldn't be over twenty, younger than Parola by several years, at least) worked with confidence and deliberation.

Tammy marveled at her kind smile and how she wasn't afraid to make eye contact. Normally, on the rare occasion that someone set foot on her property, eye contact was avoided if possible. Who wanted to lock eyes with the crazy lady?

Tammy wrote *kind* with her index finger in the dirt.

"What did you write?" Alice asked.

Surprised that Alice noticed, Tammy wiped at the dirt, erasing all signs of the word. The ease with which she erased the word stunned her. She'd. Erased. A. Word.

Tammy stared at the ground, then at her dirty hand, disbelieving. "Oh, nothing. It's a nervous habit, that's all."

"I chew my cheek when I'm nervous," Alice said. "Sometimes, I make it bleed. I'm trying to stop." Alice poured something onto a gauze pad. "This is going to sting a bit."

Tammy nodded, then winced.

"So, what do you do for a living?" Alice asked as she placed a large bandage on Tammy's knee.

"I'm a freelance writer."

"Oh, yeah? What kind of stuff do you write?"

"I used to write for magazines. Now it's all online. Parenting articles were my specialty, but now I focus on women's midlife issues." Oh, goodness. How ridiculous she sounded to her own ears. Parenting? She'd failed miserably. And midlife issues? If anyone had issues, it was her. Heck, she was the poster child for issues. They were literally piled up in her house.

What a joke. Tammy began laughing. Poor Alice. The girl didn't know what to do. Perhaps they hadn't covered mental breakdowns in her program yet.

Soon, of course, the laughter turned back into tears.

And there squatted patient Alice. "You weren't crying because you hurt yourself, were you?"

Tammy shook her head. "I'm in such a mess."

Alice handed her a tissue from the first-aid kit. "How so?"

"It's too embarrassing."

Tammy couldn't believe what happened next. Alice sat back against the tree, removing her disposable gloves and tossing them near her feet. "Try me."

"Look, you seem like a lovely girl, especially coming over here to check on me when no one else would," Tammy paused, and took a deep breath, "dare set foot on my property, but—"

"But nothing. We're neighbors."

"But we don't know each other."

"Not yet."

Tammy wondered if a camera was hidden somewhere. Why else would Alice be talking to the crazy woman on Oak Street? She felt almost as humiliated as on the day with David Pepperman. But there was no malice on Alice's face. "You are a stubborn one, aren't you?"

"That's what they tell me."

So, as sunlight filtered through the rustling leaves, and the bees buzzed on a nearby weed, Tammy decided to take a chance. "In a nutshell," she began, "I have to clean up my house or it will be condemned."

"So, what are you going to do?" Alice asked. That was it—a simple question. No visible shock, no, "Ew, gross, how dirty is it?"

"That's all you're going to say?" Tammy asked. "Surely, you've heard about me from the other neighbors."

Alice shrugged. "I like to make up my own mind. Making a snap judgment about someone is too easy."

Tammy gave her a long blink and shook her head. How could someone so young be so wise? Perhaps she had hit her head, and this was all a hallucination.

The pain in her knee and the scrapes on her arms said otherwise. She fingered the bandage. No, she wasn't imagining it.

"I don't want to move," Tammy finally admitted. "But change is hard. I don't think I can do it. Actually, I know I can't. I've tried before. It didn't make a difference."

The threats from Hal rang loud in her ears: "If you don't throw this junk away, I'm leaving." He'd repeated it often enough through the years, and one day he followed through, taking Parola with him.

"Did you get professional help?"

"No." Oh, for goodness' sake, why was Tammy baring her darkest secrets to this stranger from next door? By escaping the boxes, had she somehow wriggled herself into a new dimension? One where the sun was shining and people were nice to her?

Alice's voice penetrated her thoughts. "Maybe you weren't ready then. Maybe you are now."

Tammy wasn't so sure. The idea alone of getting rid of her life, her love, caused immediate panic. "I don't know." She buried her head in her hands. "I can't let them go. They're all I have."

"Let what go?"

"My words. Everything I've ever written is stacked up in that house. Without them, I am nothing. Without them, I am powerless." She was right back in Mrs. Findlay's math class, watching David's smug face turn to embarrassment. She'd cherished the moment when the tables had turned—after years of torment, she'd hurt someone back.

Was that the legacy she'd built her life on? Pain?

"Wow," she said.

"What?" Alice asked.

"I was thinking that if I do get help, I have a lot to unpack."

Alice began laughing, then Tammy realized the irony of what she'd said, and joined in.

When the laughter subsided, Alice reached across and gave Tammy a squeeze on the arm. This kid was pure gold. The touch was so warm and comforting to someone who'd been alone for so long that Tammy nearly broke down again.

"Thank you."

"No problem. It's good to practice."

"No, I mean, well yes, but not only for the bandage, for sitting here with me today. Talking. I don't think I've ever needed anyone more, and there you were, peering over the fence."

"Sometimes, timing is everything," Alice replied.

Tammy nodded. *Timing.* Surely, if ever there was a time to get help, this was it. Did she have the strength? Maybe, maybe not, but soon.

Perhaps connecting with Parola would give her strength. She'd written her daughter hundreds of letters. Never mailed, simply stacked in a box somewhere. But what good were they sitting there, collecting dust?

But what good were they sitting there, collecting dust?

Had she actually thought that? She trembled with the realization.

"Are you okay?" asked Alice.

"Fine. I think. I'm not sure. It's been... a day." For the first time in years, decades even, Tammy saw hope. A flash, a tiny spot glittering at the end of a long dark, scary tunnel, but it was there, nonetheless.

She closed her eyes, picturing the stacks of journals filled with her thoughts and her dreams, her heartaches, and disappointments. Could she live without all her beloved fountain pens and calligraphy tools? Even the broken ones had sentimental value. She'd used them to practice until her script was textbook perfect.

She couldn't toss those into the trash like garbage. Surely no one would make her do that. But the old grocery lists from when she still left the house? Notes from research conducted twenty years ago? Well, she could part with those. Couldn't she?

The world tilted and spun. She must have leaned into Alice, because the girl stood. "I'll be right back," she said, and exited the backyard without waiting for Tammy to reply.

She returned with a sports drink. "Drink it," Alice insisted. "It's full of electrolytes."

Tammy nodded and took a sip. It was both sweet and salty, but she drank it all down, not realizing how thirsty she was.

"Thank you," she said. Then added impulsively, "I'm wondering if I could borrow something. Two things, actually. Your lawn mower and a weed whacker."

Not quite ready to tackle the inside of the house, sitting under the tree made her realize how much she had missed being outside. Perhaps if she cleaned up the front yard, her daughter would visit. They could sit on the front porch and drink lemonade.

"Absolutely," Alice said. "I'll help, too."

"I can't ask you to do that. You've done so much already."

"That's what friends are for, right?"

Friends? They'd started the afternoon as mere neighbors. Was it that simple for the young, or had Tammy forgotten how to make friends? "Yes, yes, it is."

"I'll go get them right now," Alice said, standing and holding a hand out to Tammy.

"Now?" Beads of sweat formed along her hairline.

"Why not? It's not too hot today, and I have the time. What about you?"

Tammy hesitated. She hadn't worked for months. All she had was time. *Just do it.* "Yes, me too." She accepted Alice's extended hand and the help up. Her body ached—yup, the bruises were forming.

"Perfect."

While locating her shoes by the back door, Tammy caught her reflection in the door's window, and the sight of it nearly changed her mind. *I look deranged. Feral.* But unlike other times, she didn't retreat into her word world. Instead, she pulled an old baseball hat of Hal's off the rack in the hall and dusted it off by whacking it against her thigh. She tugged it on. Her hair, a wild nest beneath it. So what? She was cutting the grass.

It was not an easy job. Alice began edging the yard with the weed whacker, but the grass was so deep, Tammy worried the girl might trip, fall, and never be seen again.

Tammy set the lawnmower on the highest setting, but with the grass higher than her knees, it stalled out more than once. She wiped perspiration from her brow, watching Alice work in an odd, random pattern.

"What are you doing?" she yelled over the noise.

Alice laughed and turned the weed whacker off. "I'm just goofing around trying to cut out A for Alice before we mow over everything." Her hand flew up to her mouth. "Oh Tammy, I hope you don't think I'm making fun of you."

Tammy shook her head. "Don't worry." She wasn't offended. Quite the opposite. Tammy was intrigued. What if she cut out a letter then mowed over it? It would be good practice. No doubt any professional psychiatrist would've shaken their head. But none were there. She'd already erased one word in the dirt and survived.

Yes, she liked the idea. "Can I try?"

Alice passed Tammy the weed whacker, and Tammy proceeded to cut out *A and T*. She'd attempted an upright, modern, sans-serif font, and it turned out a right old mess. Yet, each movement of the weed whacker, each shape, each letter taking form, had pleased Tammy to no end.

"There," she said when finished. Beads of sweat ran down her face, her hands ached, her heart raced, and her back hurt. She was in more pain than she'd experienced in years, but also more alive. "Go onto the porch and see if you can read it."

She watched Alice leap up the stairs with the grace of a gazelle, then followed. Her footsteps loud and clumsy in comparison.

"I'm sorry," Alice said. "I can't read it."

"Me neither. What a mess!" Tammy laughed. "But now comes the hard part." Taking a deep breath, Tammy descended the stairs and picked up the weed whacker one more time, ignoring the protest from her back. Her hands shook, and briefly, she thought she might be sick, but then she heard Alice cheering her on. Inspired, she walked across the letters, swinging the weed whacker back and forth, like a scythe—or so she imagined, never having once used a scythe.

With some of the grass now shorter, she heard the lawnmower start up. And somehow, *somehow*, they finished the lawn. Together.

"Sorry, Tammy, but I have to go," Alice said, checking the time on her phone. "Today was unusual, but I had a good time, you know? I'm glad to have met you."

"Me too," said Tammy. "Your..." dare she say it? "...friendship has helped me. Immensely." Truly the understatement of the year.

"Then my work here is done." Alice took a stage bow, then wrapped Tammy in another hug. "I have a younger brother. He's 14. I bet for some pizza and a bit of cash he'd cut the backyard."

"Tell him he's hired," Tammy replied, knowing her aching back would thank her.

Alice gave a quick wave, then picked up the weed whacker and dragged the lawnmower home.

What would Alice's parents think? For one thing, they'd be grateful for not living next to an eyesore.

Which was exactly what her house was.

Even though the cut grass was a major improvement, it revealed so much more work to be done. The so-called flowerbeds grew nothing but weeds, the pathway needed power washing and edging, and the porch could use a fresh coat of paint for starters. But for the first time in far too long, Tammy wanted to do those things. Or, at the very least, hire someone to do them.

At one time, her house had been full of familial love and joy. Perhaps it could be again. She closed her eyes and imagined a freshly painted front door and porch. There'd be flowers in planters and a small table and chairs where she and Parola would sit and catch up.

She could plant lavender and daisies in the flowerbed and a climbing rose on the trellis, just like her mother had. Those pink roses had bloomed all summer long. What was the name of the variety?

Alice.

Tammy stilled. Surely this was a coincidence—but wow, one too powerful to ignore.

With determination, Tammy walked around to the back door. Inside was dark and stuffy, but the comforting presence of her words filled her. How could they not? They were her life and had been for so long, but with help, she might regain some control. The thought was daunting, but she vowed to try.

She'd journal about it, of course. The situation called for a brand-new notebook, and she'd write with a fountain pen in brown ink, as it was a warm color and not as harsh as black. Oh! Perhaps she'd start a blog, sharing her triumphs and failures. Maybe she could help others in similar circumstances. She could print the posts and hang them from—Nope! Before doing that, she'd have to throw away her printers.

All of them? Maybe she'd keep one.

Just take one step at a time, she told herself. *That's a tomorrow problem.*

Ignoring the mess of the fallen boxes, she carefully wound her way into the living room to her desk. Opening her browser, she searched for the local garden center. In its search box she typed "Alice Climbing Rose."

About Janet Koops

A former librarian, Janet is a happily married empty-nester who writes full-time from her home just east of the Rocky Mountains in Colorado. When she is not writing, she can typically be found hiking with her Alaskan Husky. Janet is a hopeless romantic who loves writing about complex women, their emotional journeys, and the healing power of love.

For more information about Janet and updates, go to: https://janetkoops.com/

The Irish Library in Kilkenny

CHRISTY MATHESON

In Irish mythology, Fionn mac Cumhaill (Finn McCool in English) rescued and married a powerful princess, Sadhbh (Saba), who was trapped in her deer form. A sorcerer called "the Dark Man" pursued Sadhbh, forcing her to hide as a deer, until Fionn's hunting hounds (who were also the children of his aunt) found and protected her. Sabhdh was able to regain her human form as Fionn's bride, but the Dark Man did not forget her. Taking on Fionn's shape, the Dark Man tricked Sabhdh. Once again, she took her deer form and this time escaped into the Peaceful Valley. In Irish folklore, the Veil—between the human and Fae world, between one time and another, between human and animal—is as thin as walking through a misty woods. You never know what is around a bend in the path.

Some years later, Fionn and his warriors found a child, Oisín (which means "little deer") in the place where Sabhdh had vanished.

Oisín grew up to be a great bard and warrior, and features in one of Ireland's most famous folktales.

Meanwhile, Fionn remarried, fell in love with yet another woman, and remarried. He is Ireland's greatest hero and has left an indelible mark on their culture and geography.

Sabhdh is never again mentioned .

What happened to the young woman who was forced to sacrifice everything in order to protect her unborn child?

My feet hit the grass hard, and I stumble to my knees. Human knees, human balance. I thought the Dark Man would leave me alone if I didn't try to go home. I thought I was done running, but—

Never mind, it's fine now! I rub my palms down my skirt, gasping for breath. Look, I'm back in the...

Actually, now that I look, I have no idea where I am. But it's fine. There's people standing around, talking quietly to each other. They look a little—well, bedraggled, maybe, and definitely cold—but perfectly calm. So it's definitely somewhere fine.

"It's fine, little plum," I mutter, rubbing my belly. I'm sure that's a happy kick. He could probably feel my pounding heart, but now everything's settling down. Making room for him. We're fine.

I sidle across the lawn. There's a bunch of young women standing about, their breath making puffs of steam as they chat.

I tumbled in over the fence, and on the far side of the grass looms a big wooden castle. The girls glance at me and no one seems to mind, but I'm used to being silent and ready to jump in my deer form. I'm wearing clothes that I've never seen the likes of, so maybe in all that running I've popped out in another time a *long* ways away. I've never managed that before! How fun! I double check that my shape is all the way normal, no leftover hooves or anything, and explore my new clothes.

My cloak is short, wool, and threadbare, in a color blue I've never seen before. Underneath I have—the words come to me as I examine them—a jumper with holes in the cuffs, a flowered blouse with a Peter Pan collar, and a skirt. How adorable! At least, I assume it is, because I love the way the other girls look!

But most of them are carrying baskets, and I haven't got anything. My eyes prickle with tears and I almost stamp my foot. I want to stay! I need to fit in!

I'm being irrational. I would scold the girls for giving in to their temper like that, but—wherever this is, I *need* to stay.

Very well. I won't let missing the basket bother me; I can figure out what to do. I take a breath, let it out on a smile, and move closer to a girl in a green coat. Her face is round and kind-looking, although her cheeks are a little sunken.

She smiles back at me. "Six more minutes. I don't know if I'm eager for them to open the doors, or afraid of being sent home."

"Me too." I have no idea what's inside or who would send us home, but I've barely talked to anyone for months and I am *highly* agreeable by now. I've been alone in Peaceful Valley for so long! This time, I leapt through the Veil as much as I could, hither and yon—my deer self is a little chaotic—hoping that I could land somewhere too far for him to find me.

"I'm Mary Catherine." She smiles, and her whole face lights up. "I won't ask you what you're studying, because everyone does and it's so dull."

"I'm Saba." Apparently I'm supposed to take her outstretched hand. I'm highly relieved I don't have to explain this "studying" because I know nothing about it—and she's not mentioning my belly, either.

She bobs our hands up and down. "That's a good old-fashioned name. Would you like some coffee? It's weak, but hot."

I agree, because it is awfully chilly standing here on the damp lawn. Other people are stamping their feet and drinking from shiny cups like what Mary Catherine hands me. I sip tentatively. Hm. This "coffee" is a powerful herb, nothing the likes of which grows in Ireland.

She asks about brothers and sisters, and I can talk about my family and ask about hers, all the while figuring out what her world is like and not giving away the secrets of mine.

Except it's not my world any more. It must be more or less the same place, because deer can run fast but not very far, but it's very far from my own time. Whenever I try to visit my family, the Dark Man tracks me down, and he will go after them next. I mustn't go back again, ever. Loneliness and panic throbs through me, but I try to smile.

"Oh." Mary Catherine touches my hand. "Did you lose someone in the war, too?"

I swallow the lump in my throat and nod. Certainly. War. That's a good explanation. "What about you? Your...brother?" That's the right age for war, for us.

She clucks and shakes her head, but I can tell she's angry about something. "Two of them. Sneaked to England and joined the Canadians. Paddy was lost at Rhineland and Paul made it home, but now they're treating him as a traitor. It's not right, it isn't!"

"That's so true. It's not right at all!" Highly agreeable, that's me.

A man in a black suit comes out the front door, and everyone on the lawn snaps to tense, fearful attention before he even rings the bell. We all move a few steps closer, although Mary Catherine and I are on the far side of the group, so I have time to figure out what's happening.

I don't want to be sent away. I can't be sent away! I'll clean their house, I'll nurse their wounded, I'll do anything if they don't send me away!

I keep our conversation going as I look around. The building is so large it must be a castle, although it's not like one I've seen before and the wood facade is hardly going to repel any attack. There are pointy bits over the windows and boards carved into curlicues, so this part is meant to be decorative. I like the colors. But Mary Catherine said her brothers went *away*, so maybe there isn't war in Ireland any more. The man is standing in some sort of ante-room, with a roof but no walls, laying out papers and things on a table. When he beckons the first women come up.

Sometimes, he passes them something and they go inside. Other times, he shakes his head and they go away, back down the path and into the woods. I have to get into the house. I *have* to! What's the right thing to say?

All the way across that wide, chilly lawn, chatting with Mary Catherine and some other girls, laughing at their jokes, sharing coffee and crusty blaa buns, I'm arguing with myself: will I offer to sleep with the man if he lets me stay? Well, probably he's just a servant, so I should indicate that I'm willing to sleep with the king, whoever he is.

On the one hand, I'm still technically married. During the daytime I'm convinced that Fionn will rescue me, but at night I'm becoming increasingly certain that he's not coming. I'm just a mná feasa, an herb woman, who can shift into a deer. He's a hero and a king with druids at his command, and he said he loved me and adored me and would take care of me forever. He said!

But it's been months, and he knows where I hide. Do I wait for him, or do I just use whatever powers I have to take care of myself? That's always a woman's power. Fionn and the Dark Man have been fighting over me, so maybe whatever-that-is will tempt this king, too.

My aunt, who trained us girls, used to say "beware of the edges of your power." I thought that was for other people, and if I was clever and determined then I could get through anything. But then I'm still aching with love for Fionn, and this baby is weighing me down, and I am just *so lonely*. I am at my edge, about to fall into oblivion.

The king here probably wouldn't want to sleep with me anyways, all round with another man's child.

But I'm certainly not "studying" anything. That's how they're getting in, I hear them saying it.

We get to the front. I'm holding Mary Catherine's thermos, so I follow her up the porch steps, and then she hands me another little box and a bundle of carrots while she digs in her basket. My hands are sweaty and my heart is pounding so fast it makes the baby kick. I am fighting with my deer instincts which say "run run run!" and still debating about the sleeping-with problem.

"And what is yours?" the man asks me, paging through Mary Catherine's papers. His voice is surprising, sing-song in a completely different cadence. "You're working on the project together?"

Mary Catherine just watches me with her wistful little smile and doesn't say that she'd never seen me before in her life.

"Yes." I have to swallow twice to get the word out.

Mary Catherine doesn't argue.

"Do you read Italian?" he asks, mildly, as though he already knows that I do.

"Yes." I lick my lips. "Very well. That's my part. Reading Italian."

I have no idea if I can read Italian, but usually that's part of slipping back into the human world—you arrive with the clothes and the language that you need. Their words are unfamiliar in my mouth (English, my new-memory tells me) but I'm doing just fine, so I will convince my power that I also need to read Italian *very very much thank you.*

"Good luck." He holds out two ribbons, and I can tell from Mary Catherine's little gasp that this is what we wanted. "I am pleased see the results of that paper when you get it done."

The inside of the castle is built out of wood, too, with glowing things on the walls. Mary Catherine passes the carrots to a servant woman, who directs us to a room where we hang up our cloaks.

Alone, Mary Catherine giggles and squeezes my hands. "We did it! I was so scared I thought I was going to faint!"

I can't help it, I bounce up and down despite the weight of my belly. Her giggle sets of an avalanche of my own—it feels so good! To be together! A friend! A girl!

"Good thing he let us by," I say. "That stinky old man! Why would he keep us out of the nice castle!" My indignation swells as I remember how I let in everyone who needed shelter, especially if they were cold. "We're both hard-working and pretty and—how long do we get to stay?"

Mary Catherine gives me a queer look and pulls her hands away. "It's for the whole semester. But it's not about being pretty."

Maybe it's good I didn't offer to sleep with the king. Although if the other girls don't care about being pretty, maybe that gives me an advantage. I need any advantage I can get, and I'm usually considered nice-looking.

"Why would he keep us out?" I'm more subdued, but still quite sure of myself. "If people are requesting shelter, then they are obligated to give it. And a servant shouldn't send them away!"

"Mr Fabbrini isn't a servant." Mary Catherine hangs her cloak, not looking at me. "And I think he has the perfect right to decide who can study in his library, given that he's spent the last twenty years bringing the books over from Italy. It's one advantage of Ireland being officially neutral, I suppose. He could get back and forth."

She sounds bitter. I find a coat-hook and try to deduce why, so I can get her to like me again, although I'm pretty stuck on how Ireland could be neutral. In a war? In all the times I've ever seen, Ireland is good at war. Really good. I decide to go with that.

"At least your brothers were brave heroes," I say. "You can be proud of them!"

She rewards me with a tentative smile, so apparently this is the right direction.

"War is always tragic"—I sense this is what she believes, so I say it—"but it is better to fight for one's family and die in glory, than for a young man to stay home cowering in fear. Your brothers will be forever showered in honor for their sacrifices!"

This is a perfectly normal sentiment, but Mary Catherine seems to find it slightly shocking.

"It's over now," she says. "Let's get to work."

That reminds me that I have no idea what we're doing here. I follow her down the hall, which is cluttered with boxes of bandages and medical supplies. The bottles are different, but I still recognize them as medicine. Some of the doors are open, and inside the rooms are dark and dusty. They have plenty of room for everyone who needs shelter!

Mary Catherine pushes open the worn double doors at the end of the hall, and we both pause in stunned silence.

So far, everything in this time has seemed fancy but worn out. This—this room has been cared for.

It is as large and tall as a Great Hall, but rectangular and still made of wood. There are eight tables in two rows down the center, where women and older men are taking notes while they sort through books. All behind us and the two long walls are covered with shelves and shelves of books, all the way to the ceiling so far above us. The ground floor has rolling ladders so people can climb to the upper shelves, and then there are two balconies encircling the room as the books go higher and higher. The far wall is all windows, with chairs and potted plants below.

"Here it is." Mary Catherine sighs. "Everything we've ever dreamed of!"

"Amazing," I agree.

If this is what she was dreaming of—not food or bedrooms—then I can see why that Mr Fabbrini fellow was turning people away, because it's pretty full. Mary Catherine and I search all through the room looking for a place to sit, and finally settle in a little nook by the windows. We have comfortably padded thrones and good-smelling plants leaning over our heads, but only a little round table. The others need a great deal of room for their books, so I'm not sure how we'll fit Mary Catherine's project. Whatever it is. Hm.

"How can I help?" I don't dare sit down. I need to show her how useful I am. "I can do anything you ask. I'll make it go faster. I can write very neatly. I can..." I have no idea what I can do. The last time I was hiding from the Dark Man, I stayed with monks for a while, and I could read and write in their time. We lived in a round tower with a ladder we could roll up, which is very different from an entire castle made out of burnable materials.

Mary Catherine is studying a piece of paper from the table. "This is map of the sections. Here, and here. Anything on Lorenzo di Medici." She sighs, but sadly this time. "Can you really read Italian?"

"Yes." If I can't—I will pretend to need to pee and duck back into the Veil and convince it to take me somewhere they speak Italian and the Dark Man will chase me and I will race back really fast but keep the Italian. Or...something.

She sighs again. "I used to. My grandfather used to make me practice, but everything is so busy, and he's getting a little"—she taps her forehead—"and I just have been...lazy, they call it. But Saba!"

She looks at me, stricken, and I sink into the chair and take her hand.

"They don't understand how hard it is, my grandfather and his brothers. They don't understand that the scholar's life is gone. It's all trying to keep the house tidy without servants and shop on ration coupons and help with the children."

"I understand. Oh, Mary Catherine, I understand!" Not that "ration coupon" part, but the loss of everything we were raised for. How much time it takes to prepare food and drink. How exhausting it is when you can't think or sing or tell stories, just caught in the logistics of functioning for day after day.

"I started this project before the war. I studied in London." Mary Catherine smiles weakly. "I can still read Italian, but I'm so slow. My parents have lost so much, Saba." She pulls one hand away to brush some tears. "I can't bear to disappoint them on this, too. All the boys are gone, and I have to finish my grandfather's research. I have to!"

Her mission sounds as important as escaping the Dark Man. I've lost my family, but I, too, would do anything to make them proud—to give them one more thing to show that I love and honor them.

"Well." I stand up and brush down my skirt. "Let's go! Let's see what we can do when we work together!"

Maybe I make a good scholar, too. This is fun! I like going up the little spiral stairs and around the balconies. I like figuring out how to organize all the books and notes with only our little tiny table and a bunch of plants. I even like wheeling the ladder back and forth and climbing up to fetch books from the upper shelves, although people keep giving me odd glances and eventually start blocking my way. I am perfectly fine climbing a ladder with a big belly! It's much easier than trying to escape the Dark Man, and much more interesting than just being in the Peaceful Valley by myself, week after week after *week*.

At mid-day, the housekeeper comes over and rings the bell, and Mary Catherine and I follow everyone else to a different big room with different tables, where we serve ourselves stew. I am so happy with this new castle and all these new things to think about, I'm ready to make new friends too. I smile at a girl standing off to the side in a brown jumper, who glances at my figure and her defensive expression melts into a reluctant smile. I don't want to talk about my belly, so I ask her lots of questions instead, about cooking and tea and cleaning up muddy footprints and other things that women have in common across the ages. Another couple women turn to answer, and soon we're all chatting and laughing. It sounds like Alice has been living on the west coast for the last few years, and other women give her advice about living here that I'm thankful to hear, because I'm from this place but not this time, but it makes Alice's mouth purse up like she's eating green berries.

Mary Catherine hangs back, with that little smile but her shoulders hunched. I link my arm through hers (that's what people do here), and my mind runs faster than a deer remembering which people have questions that Mary Catherine can answer, and vice versa, and I ask the right things so soon she is involved in the conversation too. By the time we all sit down, Mary Catherine uses her full-sunshine smile a few times, and the formerly grumpy Alice is sharing tips for cleaning windows.

The housekeeper comes by with a tray of buns. They're kind of small, and she gives each person one, which they eat carefully. I have figured out by now that this is "rationing," and there is never quite enough to go around. That's fine, I can—

She puts two on my plate.

"Oh, thank you, but you made a mistake." I smile and hold one out.

The housekeeper clucks and shakes her head. "Mangia per due, signora."

It takes a moment, like the books, as though the magic is having trouble giving me two languages at once. But I don't need to understand the words to know she is saying I am eating for two, and I'm flustered.

"Not really." I'm still holding out the bun. "Someone else needs it. I'm not..." The baby kicks me, reminding me that we really are hungry. There are gardens in Peaceful Valley, and I can switch to my deer form and graze, but I haven't eaten things like bread and meat since Fionn—

Alice puts her hand over mine, directing the bun back to my plate. "You're hungry. Just eat it."

I rub my belly. "He's still very small. Do you want half?"

Alice pushes the plate back towards me. "Fine then. When he's a fat baby and nursing all day, we'll give you three buns." She begrudges me a half-smile and lowers her voice. "Mine is two years old now. Big enough to stay with my mum while I'm here."

"You moved back to stay with your mum?" I guess.

Alice's spoon freezes for a moment. "My husband was in the Reserves. When he was—well." She pokes her soup. "I started university, before I married, and Mum figured at least I could finish my research. So we moved to Kilkenny, her and me and little Johnny."

I understand; I don't want to talk about Fionn, either. It's ridiculous how being with child makes a woman cry all the time. Foolish. I blink back sudden tears, stirring my own soup fiercely.

"Mary Catherine, your carrots!" I exclaim. "They're in the soup. And Alice brought onions. And you—"

My table-mates are nodding, the chattier ones explaining that if they live in the country, they keep gardens, and it's easier to share.

"I know what's in the forest!" I glance out the far windows, desperate. "It's spring, there are fresh things. I'll gather them for the soup tomorrow! It will be good! I can go after lunch..."

"I thought we were working," Mary Catherine says.

"We are. Maybe then—"

"Saba, it's raining," Alice says. "You don't have to go."

"But I want to bring something!" I *need* to bring something!

"We all know how to forage the healthy things from the woods," Bridget says. "You don't have to bring anything."

My heart is pounding, but I make myself smile and shrug. I press one hand on top of my belly. *Quiet down, little plum. We'll be fine. I'll take care of you. See, I'm eating two buns.*

That feels like a foot pressed against my hand, which just reminds me how big he's getting. He'll come to the world in a few weeks, and I really don't know what I'll do then. I've helped many women through labor, which can be hard, so I figure that I'll take my deer form for the birth itself. But I know we'll have to shift back soon after, and...

That's the part where there are always women around. No one I've ever known has to take care of a newborn alone. No one...

I shake my head and laugh at a joke Bridget is telling. I wonder what hopes and tragedies brought her to this ramshackle wooden castle with its enormous room of Italian books. I join in the laughter, although my heart is rushing so hard I can barely hear the story.

I shouldn't worry, because Fionn will come back for me before the child is born. He heard the prophecy that our child would be a great bard, he knew when the baby was due. Maybe he's just a little delayed.

A son is even more important than I am. Surely he's coming for us.

We work all afternoon in the library, the rain sluicing down the windows. I have retrieved enough books on Lorenzo di Medici's court to keep us busy for weeks, and now I follow Mary

Catherine's directions and look for mentions of musicians. That is her family's project. They are all musicians and scholars, tracing how this one patron affected musical progress in the Cinquecento.

I like music, too. I want to offer to sing for Mary Catherine. Maybe I could visit her grandfather, who apparently can't leave the house any more, and sing for him. Maybe he would like that. Maybe he would think my kind of music is interesting. But I don't say any of that, because I don't want to talk about myself and sound too eager and too demanding. I just go through the books, one after another. I put in little tiny strips of paper at any of the parts we should go back and read carefully, like Mary Catherine tells me to.

This is going to take forever! Do all these people really plan on sitting in a library for this long?

Wait. That's a good thing. I just have to stay useful and I can stay too. Talking at lunchtime is better than never talking to anyone at all.

Where am I going to sleep? As I walk around the library to fetch things, I hear snippets that people are intending to go back to their families at night, but they plan to return in the morning. When I use the toilet, I loop through the dark and dusty extra rooms to peer out the windows. There's some outbuildings on the south side of the house. I could sleep in a woodshed. Or the stable—it's warm in a stable. That's basically like my cave in Peaceful Valley, so it will be fine.

Except I spent years stocking my cave with all the things a proper house needs, just in case. And it doesn't get cold in Peaceful Valley—or at least, not that cold. But I had two entire blaa buns for lunch, along with the soup, so I will be full enough to last all night. I'll just go out with the other girls, and slip away on the path and return to one of the sheds. I've already noticed that they barely have any servants here; that's part of their problem. No one will notice me.

I come back to the library in time to hear a sound like a dull avalanche. Alice is standing back against the wall, arms around herself. Her books have gone sliding and tumbling every which way, papers floating down on top of the mess on the floor. The person next to her had set a ruler on the table between them, with their own books piled carefully on their side of the ruler. Everyone nearby is carefully ignoring Alice's scowl, but I know this type of anger is really just to cover up worse types of feelings.

"What are you working on?" I whisper, so not to bother the person with the neat desk. "I'm good at sorting. Just tell me and I can help."

"John Donne's poetry," she whispers back. "But aren't you reading for Mary Catherine?"

"I can do both," I assure her. I ask some more questions, and start making useful piles, including rearranging just a few decorations on the shelf behind her so I can stack extra books there.

Once I get started, Alice passes me books and pages, telling me the categories. "Thanks, y'know. I don't—don't know what came over me."

"It's fine. I like working out the patterns. It's why I like people, too." Whoops, I didn't mean to say that last part.

"I'm better at books than people," Alice admits. "Although you wouldn't know it today. There, that's good enough to be going on with."

I squeeze her hand and hurry back to Mary Catherine. I was gone a long time.

"I'll go double fast on this batch," I assure her.

She gives me that funny look again. "It's not a race; just take your time. And I'm not upset that you helped Alice, if that's what you're wondering."

But when Mr Fabbrini starts circulating through the library, my heart tumbles faster than my deer feet can gallop. I press the top of my belly. That's another funny thing about being pregnant; my heart goes faster than usual.

I'm useful, I think very loudly in my head. Who knows if magic works this way, but I'll try. I'm very useful, and very pretty, and I absolutely love Italian madrigals and I will make a great contribution to scholarship if I just can stay and work in this library.

Finally, he comes and stands by our little table, hands clasped behind his back. I dart glances at him while Mary Catherine continues to make notes. Although his hair is still dark, his face is older than I had first thought. His suit is fine wool and well pressed, but there are little mending stitches around the cuffs and the buttonholes.

I try to keep my eyes focused on the Table of Contents in front of me, so he won't suspect that I'm anyone other than another ordinary scholar.

Mr Fabbrini asks Mary Catherine about her grandfather, and some place in London, and then they discuss Lorenzo di Medici. My heart has almost settled down when he turns to me.

"And you, signora? I don't believe I caught your name this morning, in all the rush."

I realize, suddenly, that I don't know the naming conventions of this time. Should I use my father's name, or Fionn's? My house?

"Forgive me, Mr Fabbrini," Mary Catherine says. "Please let me introduce my friend, Saba…" She peters out, perhaps also realizing she is missing half my name.

"What an unusual name!" says Mr Fabbrini. "How is it written?"

Mary Catherine writes it for him, which is just as well, because I don't know which spelling they use either.

"Sa-ba," says Mr Fabbrini, the syllables precise and sharp in his accent.

I wriggle uncomfortably, because that's wrong. Mary Catherine speaks English, but she says it the right way, the second part sliding into the first, like a breath, a caress. Sahhhvvvv.

"It's an ancient name here," Mary Catherine explains. "The Catholic names have been popular in this century, but this is an old-fashioned Irish name. In ancient times, we had a Queen Saba."

Mr Fabbrini leans forward, making a little gesture for her to continue. I want her to say more too! I was Queen Saba—or I still am? I can't go back to my castle any more, but I am still myself.

"The most famous Saba was the wife of Finn McCool," Mary Catherine says mildly.

My heart stops. Yes! Yes! Keep talking! The beloved wife, and he came and rescued her—!

Mr Fabbrini lowers his eyebrows, thinking. "I thought Una was his wife. She tricked him into making Giant's Causeway, yes? And there was Gráinne. Didn't they marry?"

Surely that is not the Gráinne who is my newest lady-in-waiting. It must be someone else by the same name.

But my Gráinne is very pretty. Very.

And what's this Una?

"He was married three times, or four, depending on the source," Mary Catherine answers, as though the number of wives is inconsequential. "Saba was the very first, and she didn't last long."

"What became of her?"

I wonder that too. Very much.

Mary Catherine just shrugs. "Not long after they married, she was tricked by the Dark Man, and just disappeared from the tales."

"She can't just—disappear!" My voice comes out harsh, although I didn't mean to say anything at all. "Does she—die?"

Mary Catherine's eyes open wide. "Her son, Oisín, is found when he's an older boy, so she must have survived. But Saba herself is never mentioned again. Surely you know the stories of your namesake?"

"Of course." I try to laugh. "I know—all—the stories." Except anything that happens after today. "I guess maybe"—my mind spins—"maybe my grandmother made up extra stories for me. Because of my name. To make me happy. I didn't know that—everyone doesn't know them."

Both Mary Catherine and Mr Fabbrini nod and say something about grandmothers and their stories. I try to smile, but my heart has escaped my chest and is pounding in my throat.

She never comes back. Fionn goes on. Three wives. Or four.

I thought he *loved* me. He knew where I was. I always went to the Peaceful Valley! He knew that!

"But that wasn't what I had come to ask." Mr Fabbrini rests his hand on the back of my chair. "We have some extra rooms upstairs, for any of the scholars who might find the trip back and forth to their homes to be too difficult to manage daily. Would either of you care to stay?"

I stare at Mary Catherine. What if I say yes?

She darts a tiny smile at Mr Fabbrini. "I need to be home to help with evening chores. But I think Saba would like to stay."

"Excellent, excellent." He taps my chair. "We will expect you for dinner, Signora Saba."

"Thank you." I manage that much. I am polite. Agreeable.

Even when my heart is beating so fast that it will soon be gone forever.

Fionn is not coming back. The prophecy is right, I will bear this baby—but I will do it alone.

And *alone* is the cruelest punishment of all. I would know.

Mary Catherine leaves soon afterwards. I ought to keep finding important passages, but I don't care at all about Lorenzo di Medici. Another man. More power. More wives. Pah!

No one is looking at me. I slip around a plant pot, long narrow leaves brushing my hair, and press myself between the greenery and the window, cold against my shoulder and cheek.

I stare into the rain and the tears slide down my face. I don't let my shoulders shudder, so no one can tell.

But they can see I've left my books. They can tell I'm not a real scholar.

It doesn't matter. I was just pretending to be one of them, anyways. I've heard my destiny, and I know I just deliver this baby and quit. No hope. No future.

No Fionn coming back for me, ever.

The baby pushes his foot into my lungs, maybe disliking the way I'm taking up his space with how I'm holding in my sobs. I push back on the top of my belly, hard. It's nasty and terrible, but right now I don't even *like* this baby. I wanted a family. I dreamed of giving Fionn a son and how much more he would adore me. All right, so I knew he was a little distracted, and it was easier to *talk* about loving me than actually spending time together. But it was going to be better. Definitely he would love me when I gave him a son.

But he doesn't. He won't.

The bell clangs on the far side of the library, and a rising tide of chatter fills the hush. I surreptitiously rub my eyes on my sleeve and put my smile back on. We're allowed to leave our books in place, so I neaten the stacks and tuck my notes in with Mary Catherine's.

I won't be coming back tomorrow. What's the point, when I'm just disappearing? I'll go down the path with the others, and wave goodbye and go into the woods. My deer self has always been able to find the way back to Peaceful Valley, ever since I was a child and thought it was all a lovely way to escape my lessons. I don't need to be with other people or research Lorenzo di Medici or any of that. I'll just munch leaves and live in my comfy cave, and give birth as a deer, and raise the child until he's old enough to nudge back into the real world where his father can find him. That's all. That's my destiny. Nothing.

I pull my jumper around myself and join the throng going down the hall to the cloak room, accidentally jostling Alice.

"You!" She takes my elbow and moves us out of the crowd. "Do you have a church of your own around here? I thought not. Well then, you're coming with Mum and Johnny and I to church and spending Sunday night. We'll have a fine craic before work starts again on Monday. Do you sing?"

I meant to demur, but the direct question startles me into answering. Of course I sing.

"Good! Your voice sounds like you do. It'll be great."

"But I'm...I'm not sure..." I wasn't going to be here by Sunday. Or ever again.

Alice shakes her head ominously. "I've been in your shoes, having a baby far from home. You need to be around a family. We're"—sorrow flits through her stern expression—"just a little family, but we're something. You spend Sundays with us. It's a rule now."

"Can you raise a baby without his daddy?" I didn't mean to say that. I didn't even know I was thinking it. It's terribly rude, and of course I've known plenty of daddies killed in wars, we just all used to be in the same big house and we would all—

"Oh, Saba." Alice glowers. "We do what we have to. You can too."

I guess I do have to raise this baby until he's old enough to go back. That's what the stories said; I'm not done yet. Maybe it's too early to give up.

Alice sighs. "It's so annoying, isn't it, how when you're with child you end up crying all the time? Ridiculous!"

It's exactly what I've been thinking all day, so I burst out giggling, and Alice chuckles along.

"Signora Saba? You come?" The housekeeper approaches us, smiling along.

Alice waves goodbye and heads into the cloak room. "See you in the morning, but Sunday at my house. You promise?"

She waits until I say it. "I promise."

That's binding, now. I follow the housekeeper obediently.

We don't eat in the hall with all the tables. We don't even eat in a dining room. Most importantly, there are no other bedraggled Irish girls here, making cheery conversation about books. It's just me.

I'm sitting in a cushy throne in front of a decorated fireplace, with a little folding table in front of me, and three Fabbrinis in the other thrones. Mr Fabbrini changed into a brown velvet jacket. His wife limps heavily, and has the pinched face of the chronically ill. There is an elder Mr Fabbrini, who must be the proper king of this castle, but he gazes into space, hums, and occasionally inserts comments which have nothing to do with the conversation but always make him chuckle.

One part of me is happy. After all, I too was raised as a princess and became a queen; although the styles are different, I am accustomed to soft carpets and beautiful art and roaring fires.

The other part knows I don't belong here. In this world, I'm meaningless. In fact, I probably don't exist.

My baby rolls, poking me with elbows and heels. He thinks we exist.

Mrs Fabbrini started by apologizing that she didn't spend any time in the library today, and now is asking her husband about the various research projects. We are all speaking in Italian, which the magic understands that I need. I gobble my food (how rude!) and press on the little heel in my side, trying to get him to calm down. *I'm sorry, little plum. You'll be a really nice baby. I'll try to be a good enough parent, even if I have to do it all by myself.*

That sounds hard. Who can be a good enough parent, all by themselves?

"Signora Saba, how did your day go? Did you find any new madrigalists?"

I startle, and stare at Mrs Fabbrini over my fork full of pork cutlet. "I put...lots of paper marks in the places to go back and read...?" Is that even an answer? Is that progress?

"You write on paper, and paper is patient," murmurs King Fabbrini, and giggles.

"Yes, papa." Mrs Fabbrini turns back to me. "Ah, silly me. This sort of research takes so long, but I am always eager to hear."

"Very long," I agree. "I marked so many passages."

They all nod, and comment on the reading time, and whether they brought the right books from Italy. I chew my pork, more and more confused.

I understand that Mary Catherine wants to honor her grandfather. I understand that Alice needs to dive into something to balance out the overwhelming grief of losing her husband. I understand that all the women yearn to prove to themselves that they are more than cleaning windows and growing carrots.

But sitting in a chair for months sounds *so boring!* I love stories, but they're best told while you're walking in the woods to collect herbs, or busy weaving!

"I shouldn't be here!" Whoops—I didn't mean to interrupt Mrs Fabbrini.

They all turn to me, even King Fabbrini's bleary eyes attentive.

"I'm sorry." I bite my lip, trying to hold back those stupid tears, and rub my baby's foot. "I'm not really a scholar. I don't belong here. You are giving me a room and all this good food, and I don't deserve any of it."

"Do you have a home near here?" Mrs Fabbrini asks gently.

"Ye-es. And I have a garden. I just..."

Everyone waits, as though what I say matters to them.

"I'm not a scholar," I repeat. "I like to sing, but I don't know anything about madrigals. It's all fake." The baby moves his foot, and I can't keep the tears back any longer. "You should send me away."

"Signora Saba." Mr Fabbrini pushes his little table aside, leaning forward to fix me with his gaze. "I have watched all day, and you are not fake. Your smiles light up the room. You are drawing the outsiders into conversation. You work tirelessly and help anyone who needs it. You are filling our little research team with a sense of camaraderie, instead of the competition which so many scholars adopt."

"Anyone could do that!" I rub my face with my napkin, trying not to be silly and maudlin.

"But they don't," Mr Fabbrini answers.

"I didn't go to college!" From listening all day, I have learned what trials these women have gone through to get their degrees. "I don't have any paperwork at all!"

Mr Fabbrini sighs. "I know that."

I am so startled that I stop crying.

He flips his hands in a broad shrug. "I let you in this morning. I saw that you had no papers, but that Mary Catherine trusted you. That was enough to give you a chance, which you—"

"Roberto." Mrs Fabbrini speaks firmly. "You speak as though Signora Saba must earn her place at our table. You know this is not the case."

"My apologies," he replies immediately.

"God has been gracious to us," King Fabbrini says. "We always have a place for those in need."

"So true, papa." Mrs Fabbrini turns to me again. "You must stay with us. This house you speak of—I am not convinced that all is well. I have seen a thing or two in my lifetime, young lady. Do not try to fool me."

I giggle through my tears and runny nose, because I'm not sure she's seen a woman who changes into a deer to run from a druid who lived two thousand years ago. I'm not sure anyone has seen it; I've just got to figure it out. Because whether or not I'm in the history books, I'm here.

"I do have a house," I say, "but I'm very lonely." And it's also cold, and it's also a cave. "And I'm not sure..." I have to take a drink of water before I can go on. "I think my husband is not coming back."

"It happens, especially in wartime," Mr Fabbrini says.

King Fabbrini nods. "Pride, envy, avarice—these are the sparks have set on fire the hearts of all men."

This time, he is the one who is correct. I knew these were my husband's weaknesses, and I suppose they have burned him up.

"You will stay with us," Mrs Fabbrini declares. "Through the winter, certainly. Then we can see what we shall see."

"I don't—I mean I can't—" I take a breath. "I shall clean for you. I will—"

"In your condition? Absolutely not."

"What can I do, then, to earn my place?"

Mr Fabbrini looks at his wife, and they both sigh and shake their heads.

"You will be yourself," Mr Fabbrini says. "You will talk with us at dinnertime, and encourage the other girls, and smile and sing and spread good cheer."

"*When* you are up to it," Mrs Fabbrini adds. "Some days, you can be the one to accept smiles and encouragement."

"The deeds you do may be the only sermon some persons will hear today," King Fabbrini says.

"That is very true," I tell him. "I am honored to dine with such a wise man."

He beams. "St Francis of Assisi," he tells me. "You liked the Dante Allighieri too, I think."

These syllables make no sense to me, so I turn back to Mrs Fabbrini. "Are you sure? In my condition, I'm asking so much, and have so little to give."

She passes a hand over her eyes. It takes a moment before she speaks, slowly. "In the last years, we have all seen so much suffering. We have lost so much, in our own country in the first war, and now so much more in our new country. We cannot solve the problems of the world, but if we retreat entirely into our own fear and suffering, then we lose our own humanity. We can save a few books from the bombing. We can open our library to young dreamers. And yes, we can share our empty shell of a house with one woman who is afraid and lonely at the most difficult time in her life."

"Please stay," adds Mr Fabbrini.

I nod, unable to find words in any language. Maybe for these people, too, the hunger of loneliness is more piercing than all the deprivations of the body.

Maybe when it's not raining, I'll take the scholars for walks to help them stay healthy. Maybe I can come up with a salve that will help Mrs Fabbrini's limp. Maybe I can learn to sing madrigals!

"Look." Mr Fabbrini nudges his wife. "She's smiling. Isn't it such a pretty smile?"

"A single sunbeam is enough to drive away many shadows," announces King Fabbrini, and this time we all laugh.

See, little plum? I rub my belly as the housekeeper brings in dessert and Mr Fabbrini refills all our glasses. *Your daddy isn't coming back, but I'll find someone to be family for you. Always. I promise.*

About Christy Matheson

When Christy Matheson is not throwing ordinary characters into fairy tales, she is busy raising five children. (Very busy.) She writes character-driven historical fiction with and without fantasy elements, and her "fresh, smart, and totally charming" stories have won multiple awards.

Christy is also an embroidery artist, classically trained pianist, and sews all of her own clothes. She lives in Oregon, on a country property that fondly reminds her of a Regency estate (except with a swing set instead of faux Greek ruins), with her husband, five children, three Shelties, one bunny, and an improbable quantity of art supplies.

Intrigued by mythological retellings? Read *The White Deer of Kildare* for the tale of Queen Saba and Finn McCool, and follow Christy's newsletter to catch Saba's next story in the "Castle in Kilkenny: Fairy Tales."

For Christy's newsletter, go to: https://sendfox.com/ChristyMatheson

The Birthday Wish

PAULETTE STOUT

Birthday candles cast a warm glow on my daughter's face as she carefully shuffled with my cake across our darkened kitchen. My husband and son started a chorus of "Happy Birthday" from their seats around the table while my mother pouted in the corner of our banquette. Nothing to be done for her grumpiness, so I refocused on my beautiful daughter.

I beamed with pride watching Bia present her creation, a carrot cake with cream cheese frosting and orange rabbit decorations. Now an adult, she had become an excellent baker, shooing me out of the kitchen on multiple occasions while baking my surprise. Logan also refused to let me help with dinner prep. My son's cooking tasted delicious as always, and I envied the fearless way he combined ingredients. Fear of failure made me a timid chef. Unfortunately, that cowardice extended to how I handled other situations in my life. Most of all, my mother.

As Bia drew nearer, I spied my son holding his smartphone to record the moment while wildly conducting with the other arm.

I leaned into my husband to whisper. "How does he move like that and keep the phone still?"

"If you shot social videos for a living, you'd be good at it too." Walt reached over and took my hand. "Happy Birthday, Naomi. I hope you know how much we love you."

I did. Their devotion tonight filled my love cup to overflowing. I didn't deserve all this attention. My family was spoiling me, unlike my critical mother, for whom I was never good enough. I scanned the candle-lit faces around the table, deflating when reaching Mom's scowl. It deepened on every happy occasion that didn't center on her. At my college graduation, my father actually handed her a jewelry gift right before photos so she'd have a smile on her face. I later wished Mom frowned. At least, that would've been for me.

Mom had been staying with us, ostensibly to escape her bathroom construction. But when it finished three weeks ago, she made no move to return home. Not a peep. If I weren't so spineless, I would have mentioned it.

But I was me.

A textbook people-pleaser who took a ten-mile hike around conflict to avoid passing through. I wouldn't raise the issue, just like I wouldn't scold her pouting at my birthday dinner.

The cake arrived, and my daughter stepped back. "Make a wish, Mom!"

"Make it good!" My son yelled, experiencing events through his cell screen.

"Make it fast," Mom grumbled. She crossed her arms and looked away, as if the dark corners of our kitchen held more appeal than her family.

Insecurity gnawed at me. Despite all my accomplishments in life, Mom would undoubtedly cut me down with one of her snarky insults. Most likely, about my candle-blowing technique.

Three puffs? What? Do you have asthma? Better hit the gym...

I cleared my mind of negative thoughts and focused on picking a birthday wish worthy of this moment. Given my superstitious nature, I had no doubt it would come true. My request to the cosmos must benefit the most people.

My husband's eager expression spurred me on.

Eyes closed while I intoned my wish: for the health and happiness of everyone around this table. That they'd have the strength to weather tough times, show themselves grace, and remember to be kind to themselves.

Satisfied, I sucked in as much air as possible to blow out the six candles surrounding the numerals for my age: 57. Cheers erupted, followed by regrets for not buying trick candles. I'd tormented the kids for years with flames that reignited despite being blown out several times. Logan and Bia plotted payback for my next birthday while I sliced hearty pieces of cake to share around the table.

"Time for the big surprise!" Walt set down his fork and rubbed his hands together in that mischievous way that meant he was up to something.

"What's going on?" I asked.

Hubby and I rarely exchanged gifts outside of the holidays. We'd focused our energies and resources on the kids. Apparently, now that they were grown and had jobs, the whole lot of them had gone rogue.

My son danced over to my side and handed me a bulging, hot pink envelope. I slipped my finger under the flap and pulled out a beautiful hand-painted card with white gardenias on a lush green background. A folded paper fell out and landed on the table. "Thank you, everyone. It's lovely."

"You need to read it." Bia retrieved the page and unfolded it in front of me.

I took one look, shocked, my gaze shifting between them for a reality check.

"Yup!" Bia bounced on the balls of her feet, clasping both her hands.

"What does it say?" My mother yelled from across the table.

The lump in my throat made it hard to speak, but I did my best. "Because of all you do for us, we have rented you a lake house for three days. You can read, boat, and swim to your heart's content. Enjoy this well-deserved vacation. Time to shower some kindness on yourself! Love, Walt, Logan, and Bia."

My heart leaped with the thrill of it all while tears welled in my eyes. Three days to myself? What a dream! But as quickly as my elation spiked, it dimmed. What would Walt do for dinners? And Mom? She was a handful. Laying her at my husband's feet would be grounds for divorce.

I scanned them for confirmation. "Are you sure?"

"If we weren't, we wouldn't have rented the house," Bia said. "You'll love it. It's on Squam Lake in New Hampshire. We've filled the fridge with your favorites. You'll leave tomorrow and will have a blast!"

Walt caught my eye, already knowing what I was thinking. Thirty-years of marriage will do that.

"Don't worry about anything here. The kids are staying to help. Logan's working remotely from here until you return." He kissed the top of my head. "Go. Have fun."

I teared up as I rose to give each a tight squeeze. "I guess this is happening!"

Bia cleared the table, chattering about the relaxing break I'd have. No shopping. No laundry. Just reheating prepared meals and roasting marshmallows in the fire pit. I could already hear the crackling flames.

With a busy life and career, I had precious little time for myself. And by little, I meant next to none. When those Instagram memes popped up in my feed, with sayings about treating myself with the kindness and grace I'd give a best friend, I withered in shame. Of anyone I knew, I treated myself the worst. But then, I'd learned from the best.

Across the table, the deep-set wrinkles on Mom's face told the story of my childhood. Her mouth bracketed with lines of disappointment. Her furrowed brows of angry-confusion, followed by biting questions. Why were my clothes so sloppy? My weight too high, then too low, then too high? How could I choose a lame profession like marketing? Why didn't I follow my father and become an attorney? And don't forget her pursed lips of distaste when food, or life wasn't to her liking. I was trained to put myself last. I was too distracted trying to win a fruitless game of measuring up.

But serving others had brought me boundless joy. It's how I'd built a loving home with Walt, parenting the way I wished I'd been raised.

My children would never wonder if they were loved or good enough.

My husband would never be neglected or unappreciated.

My friends and employers could count on me.

All this took energy. And for the first time, the weight of perfection had worn me thin. Three days to myself, completely undisturbed, would enable me to recharge.

I snapped my fingers. "I'd better email my boss and make sure the timing works."

"It's been handled." Walt stilled my hand. "She was relieved and suggested you take an extra day after you return. You're not due back at work 'til Wednesday."

Tears of relief prickled my eyes. I covered my face, embarrassed by my display of emotions. My shoulders shook.

"Mom, it's okay," Bia squeezed me tight, then Logan piled on, kissing the top of my head while Walt held my hand.

The four of us were so distracted at our end of the table that I'd completely forgotten Mom, who sat stewing in the corner. I caught Walt's attention and mouthed "mom" and rolled his eyes at her silent tantrum. At least that's better than the Christmas fiasco. Back then, she tossed all our "thoughtless" gifts in the trash and pouted in her car for three hours.

"Everything okay, Diana?" My husband asked, then tensed for impact. Mom kept a quiver of razor-sharp complaints strapped to her side like an assassin.

She sighed. "I was trying to fathom why you'd give your wife such a thoughtless gift. Sending her God knows where to be all alone in the woods? What could be worse?"

Walt blanched.

I tapped the kid's arms to release me. "Mom, you're being incredibly rude. It's a perfect—"

"You're just saying that to be polite." She laced her fingers and rested them on the table, a judge ready to pronounce her verdict. "Naomi. You can't possibly want this trip. You're just too weak to stand up for yourself."

She was damn lucky we let her hang around us given her toxic influence. When the kids were little, I once found her on the verge of divulging sacred secrets about tooth fairies and Santa Claus to their precious faces. I sprinted across the room, clamped a hand over her mouth, and dragged her away in the nick of time. What was she thinking? Crushing the starry-eyed dreams of babes? My mother that's who.

I was so pathetic, I had to escape my own home to get a break from her.

A pang of frustration sizzled inside me that my silence proved her right. I was too weak, but it wasn't my family that needed a tongue-lashing. It was her. Instead, I plastered on a smile. "Who wants more cake?"

Later in my bedroom, I scratched my head, wondering which of the clothes I had laid out would make it into my suitcase. There were so many potential activities. Boating, walking in the woods, sitting by the campfire, cuddling up with a good book. While excited for the opportunity, I'd have to repay my family's kindness afterwards. Right now, though, I needed two plastic grocery bags to wrap shoes.

I padded down our carpeted stairs to the first floor, passing the guest room. It used to be an office, but we shifted that upstairs to make it easier for Mom to stay over without having to navigate steps. Yet another way we reorganized our life to accommodate hers.

The door to Mom's room was open, clothes scattered on her bed. Had she done laundry, or was she finally packing to head home?

I stepped in. "What's all this?"

She eyed me, then returned to her dresser. "I'm coming with you."

Her words smacked me like a bucket of ice water.

First she insults the idea. Then she elbows in?

What a load of crap!

I pressed my lips tight as a lifetime of hurt and resentment thrashed inside me. Years of unacknowledged slights, ignored inconveniences, and ruined holidays demanded a champion. Someone to step up and tell my mother that her behavior was unacceptable. She shouldn't have to be told how inappropriate this was. But her packing would continue unless I stepped up.

"This is my birthday gift, not yours. And you're not coming."

I hugged myself, already feeling untethered as my words floated free. It left me exposed without my shelter of cowardice. My mom shouldn't be a threat to me, especially in my own home. But the woman who birthed me decades ago on this very day rarely showed me love. How often did she wish her womb had rejected me and spared her the trouble? And if I was such a nuisance, why did she want to spend one-on-one time with me?

Mom slapped a blouse on the bed, her skin flushed with anger. "You'll go batty out there by yourself. You need me, Naomi, and always have."

A laugh huffed out of me before I could stop it, drawing her death stare.

"Do you hear yourself? You carry on like the only competent person on the planet is you. We've done okay for ourselves, don't you think?"

A normal person would have answered me. But Mom orbited a stratosphere all her own. The longer the silence simmered, the angrier I got. How dare she treat me this way! And on my birthday no less.

I cleared my throat. I wanted every word to land with full impact.

"The only place you're going is home." My anger with her had finally overshadowed my fear.

She froze mid-fold of a cotton sweater set. "Are you asking me to leave?"

Yes, was on the tip of my tongue, but brave me scurried under the bed, pressing a "shush" finger to her lips to avoid capture.

"Look," I softened my tone. "The plan was for you to stay for two weeks, three tops. It's been nearly six. Were you planning to move in permanently?"

"The thought had crossed my mind," she said while resuming her packing. "It's obvious you need the help."

I swallowed my amusement. She created more work for me, not less. Her special food requests sent me rushing all over town trying to match the photos she texted me. Then there was the noise. Mom blasted her TV shows all day while Walt and I cupped hands over our earbuds to hear our colleagues on conference calls. Logan and Bia weren't even safe from her nastiness. I'd limited their exposure to my mother while raising them, but she'd made up for lost time during this visit. Mom spat out enough veiled insults to make my children question their futures, bodies, and relationships. With me gone for three days, she would inflict serious damage.

I had to get her out of the house. For my kids' sakes.

"Fine. We'll leave at six a.m. and eat on the road." I turned and walked away, a bottomless pit already aching in my stomach. My vacation was ruined. But I'd keep my children safe from further harm.

At least for now.

"You're not seriously going to let her go with you?" Walt said, his face a ball of confusion and hurt.

I shifted my suitcase to the floor to sit on while he zippered it. Our usual getaway routine, given what a heavy packer I was. But this time, it held no joy. "It's not what any of us want, most of all me. But she was downstairs packing. What was I supposed to do?"

"Say no, and mean it," he said.

I shook my head in defeat, emotion making my lips tremble. This is not how I expected our evening to end, given my special meal and birthday gift.

"Come here." Walt drew me into a tight squeeze, his touch a balm for my frazzled nerves. "You deserve better than this. Your mom's intrusion has to stop."

It was a one-sided argument where we agreed about everything. Except what to do about it.

As I pulled off the highway into a diner parking lot, I was so angry and frustrated that I hadn't spoken to Mom since last night. It took a while, but she finally noticed. And that's when her mood improved. From then on, she'd cheerfully pose questions, then reply on my behalf.

"Isn't it a lovely day" she'd say, then answer. "Yes, Mom, it is." On and on without a shred of shame.

Not once did she ask why I was upset. Why do that when mocking me was so much fun?

As we entered the restaurant, the hostess said to sit anywhere. I scanned the room of tables and booths and strode straight to the open stools at the counter. Facing her for a meal was a courtesy she didn't deserve. I'd rather ogle refrigerated cakes. We sat opposite a mirrored wall, but a coffee maker and other food service equipment blocked most of it.

"You expect me to sit on a wobbly stool?" Mom's face twisted in disgust as she surveyed the rotating red vinyl.

I pressed my hand into the upholstered surface and attempted to wiggle it. The stool was sturdy as an oak tree. I gestured for her to sit and took the seat beside her.

The server poured us coffee, scribbled our orders, and left.

"Naomi, you can't go the whole weekend and not speak to me. I know you did it once when you were sixteen... or was it seventeen?" She pondered for a moment, then waved her hand. "No matter. You are making me feel unwelcome."

I dropped my coffee spoon on the metal counter with a loud clank. "My family gifts me a vacation, and you force yourself in? Did you ever consider that you feel unwelcome because you are? Have you no fucking shame?"

"Don't use that language with me," Mom whisper-screamed, her eyes darting around for eavesdroppers. No one was listening, and I wish I had the luxury.

"And I didn't force myself on you. I strongly recommended it. You could have said no at any time. This is your choice."

She unfolded her paper napkin across her lap as if her word settled matters.

My normal reaction would be to let her inane thinking go unchallenged. But this weekend was all about kindness to me. That began with being honest about my feelings and needs.

"That's bullshit, and you know it. I express myself, and you disregard it all as if I haven't spoken. Like your one-sided conversation in the car. Only today it bothered you because you'd lost your 'adoring' audience." I air-quoted the last part with my fingers. I was done keeping my anger in. "Your behavior makes loving you near impossible. I'm not Dad."

Her brows furrowed, lips quivering as if silently practicing her reply before letting her vocal cords in on the fun. "What do you mean? About your father?"

How much should I share? My father had always considered Mom out of his league, and in a way, she never let him forget. To his dying day, he treated his wife like a jewel, showering her with gifts and praise. When he traveled out of town for work trips, his primary concern was that Mom had what she needed while he was away. As the only other person in the house, it was up to me to carry the load. Before and after school, I had to squeeze in all his usual chores so Mom wouldn't be burdened. Mowing the lawn. Light home repairs. Shopping for groceries. She was a porcelain doll. Dad and I drifted through the rooms of our home like ghosts, lest the sounds of our labor disturb her resting spot on the top shelf. But I was the child, not her, and deserved care and attention. I was done parenting her.

Our food arrived, and I swiveled forward, losing any momentary interest I had in addressing my mother's question. "You knew Dad best. Figure it out."

Pancakes, sausage links, and scrambled eggs lay before me, and the aroma hit every box on my breakfast bingo. I dipped my fork in. "Oh my lord, this is delicious!"

I savored my meal as Mom's went untouched.

"Naomi, stop being coy. If you have something to say about your father, spit it out."

I cranked my head in her direction. "No. I don't think I will."

The power balance between us had shifted in my favor. It was a heady, intoxicating sensation that amplified the joy happening in my mouth. I dug in, pausing for sips of my decaf latte every few bites. I almost forgot I had a tablemate when she spoke.

"Are you implying that your father loved me and you don't?"

It's telling that Mom got so close to the truth on her first try. I liked to pretend her horrible behavior was an unconscious impulse she couldn't control. But her insightful guess was a thunderclap. She understood her thoughtlessness harmed me and did it anyway. Dad had been gone for years, and here I was dusting around my yard sale find of a mother like she was a priceless treasure.

"Look at our relationship over the last 57 years. You're delusional if you think you mothered me better than I mothered you." I turned back to my breakfast. "Best eat up. I won't be doing any grocery scavenger hunts for you while we're away. Whatever's in the house is what you get, and they're my favorites."

Because this weekend was supposed to be about me.

As I sat side-by-side with the woman I was birthed to love, it occurred to me I didn't. It wasn't because I was a bad person. It's because she never earned the privilege.

I rose to go to the bathroom and had to use the men's room since the women's was under construction.

The genius idea arrived like a gorgeous sunrise.

I knew how to get my weekend back.

"Wasn't that our exit?" Mom asked as we motored along the highway.

I hummed the tune on the radio, my spirits already lifting. "I'm taking a scenic route."

We drove another twenty minutes while my mother "rested her eyes." I couldn't have envisioned a better scenario as I pulled into the driveway and cut the engine.

"We're here!" I said loud enough to jar her awake.

She smiled, stretching and looking out the passenger window to inspect the unfamiliar surroundings. Her face fell when she saw her own home.

"Why are we here?" Mom's head snapped around in a panic.

I shifted toward her, resting my left elbow on the steering wheel. "I thought about what you said at breakfast. And you were absolutely right. It was my choice to let you force your way into my birthday weekend. You're a grown woman and should know how rude and selfish it was to do that. So I've done you the favor of changing my mind."

She watched me warily. Instead of fiery determination, she clutched the purse in her lap for protection, tears clinging to her eyelashes.

Call me cruel, but I couldn't contain my glee.

I'd finally bested the person who kept me pinned to a felt board while she plucked off my wings, one by one, until I could no longer fly. Well, fuck flying. I had wheels.

I opened my driver-side door and rounded to the back to open the trunk. Her suitcase sat on top, as if I'd always known she wasn't coming to the lake. When I lifted it out and shut the hatch, Mom stood beside me. Shrunken.

"I only packed for the weekend."

"No worries."

"My car is at your house."

"I called Walt from the diner. He and Logan will bring the car and all your belongings by this afternoon." I crossed my arms, tempting her to defy me. But she bowed her head and sulked down the paved path to the front door, keys in hand. She'd already retrieved from where she kept them clipped in her purse at all times. Small blessings.

The air inside her house was dusty and stale. Mom stood in the foyer, surveying her home. I passed her, bringing the suitcase to her bedroom and placing it on the wide, flat trunk at the foot of her bed. It's where she liked it, so I extended her a nicety she'd never consider for me. That fact confirmed why reclaiming my weekend felt so right.

I returned to the dining room near the front door, where someone had arranged stacks of her mail into neat rows.

She joined me, shoulders slumped in defeat. "My neighbor was nice enough to bring it over and water the plants. I guess I have been gone a while."

Without counting, I knew there were at least 42 piles, one for each day she was with us. Mom was nothing if not organized, but the look on her face extended to overwhelm. Or something bordering on anguish. This was an expression I couldn't quite place.

She approached the table, listless, picking up one envelope, before bracing herself with both arms on the dining table, crumpling it in her left hand as her whole body wept.

I rubbed her back. "You're going to be fine, Mom. This is your home."

She spoke through sobs. "I know. I'm not sure what's wrong with me."

"Why don't you call one of your friends? Maybe Aunt Jean? They can come over and help you settle in."

"I'm perfectly capable of tidying my own house," she spat.

Yes, you are.

"Well, everything is out of the car. I best get going."

"Already?"

"The lake is waiting."

She swallowed, nodding. "I hope you have a restful time. You work hard and deserve it."

I paused, taking her in. A genuine compliment? Maybe this stunt had jarred some humanity loose. A bud of optimism bloomed that this could be a turning point for us. That Mom would ditch her negative ways and make space for joy. It was a slim chance, but better than none.

I kissed Mom's temple. "Thanks for saying that. I'll call when I get back and let you know how it went."

Out in the car, I turned over the ignition as Mom stepped onto the front step to wave goodbye.

I honked twice, then drove off for my weekend adventure.

After I arrived at the lake, I dove in for a refreshing swim. The day grew hot and sunny, as if the weather gods approved of my life-altering decision to stand up for myself. As my family said, it was well past time to show myself some of the love and kindness

I gave everyone else. That choice didn't make me less. It made me free.

Limbs slack, I floated on my back, riding the swells completely at ease. Honoring my right to respect and appreciation would reset how I approached everything. Work, family, friendships, and especially Mom.

Having me in her life was a privilege. I knew that now. My birth-debt had long since been repaid.

Yes, my mother was a selfish narcissist, but consequences were finally on the table. Avoiding them might motivate her to behave like a human. If not, we'd all be seeing a lot less of Grandma Diana.

I chuckled, thinking about my birthday wish. It came true. I shouldered the strength needed to weather a tough time with Mom, showed myself grace, and remembered to be kind to myself. All told, an impressive beginning to a new trip around the sun.

It was the life I deserved.

It was the life my family deserved.

And that was a birthday gift of kindness to myself.

About Paulette Stout

Paulette Stout is the multi-award-winning author of contemporary novels with determined heroines, romance, and a fearless social pulse. Read in 44 countries, Paulette crafts vibrant settings and authentic characters you can reach out and touch.

Her 25 book award recognitions span her four novels, What We Give Away, What Eyes Can't See, What We Never Say, and Love, Only Better, adding to her three advertising industry awards, including a MediaWeek All-Star. By day, Paulette leads content and branding at a Nasdaq-listed software company, and in her "free time" co-hosts The Best of Book Marketing Podcast.

Connect with Paulette on her website at https://paulettestout.com

Mac and Cheese Love

KIMBERLY NIXON

The doctor said the cancer was back. Sylvie had resisted returning to the oncologist. But the increasing intensity of the pain last week didn't allow her to ignore it any longer. She pulled into her driveway, carefully avoiding the large crack in the asphalt, and cut the Mini-Cooper's engine. Though she could see Wade standing at the kitchen sink, she stayed in the car to hold back time. Memories of newborn grandbabies, their recent family beach trip, and the chaotic family-focused Christmas days swirled around in her mind as if they belonged elsewhere. The diagnosis wouldn't be real until she told Wade about it.

He wore his favorite apron, which said 'Hot Stuff Coming Through'—it made him laugh more than anyone else who saw it. Apparently, he had prepared dinner, arriving earlier this afternoon from his three-day Chicago work trip. He waved and beckoned her inside, smiling as if he had forgotten about her doctor appointment this afternoon—the one she had said was routine.

She opened the car door, gathered her large purse and courage, and trudged to the front door. Wade held it open for her. "Your timing couldn't be better, Mrs. Dodd."

Sylvie smiled and inhaled the smell of pork roasting. "Ah, you made my favorite meal. Thank you, Wade."

She put her things down and hugged him as he held the mashed-potato covered wooden spoon high in the air. She didn't let go. He dropped the kitchen utensil, untied his apron, and just held her. Their conversation happened without words—he knew. Her grief moved through her body—just like the cancer had—a hint of despair at first, then full force resulting in a racking sob. Her shoulders bobbed up and down with each wail, out of control. She held her breath, then exhaled the words. "It's back. In the lining of the brain this time. There's nothing they can do."

Wade led her to her favorite wingback chair and poured a tall glass of chilled Sauvignon Blanc. He sat next to her on the edge of his La-Z-Boy, leaning forward to hold her hand. There were no words. Their yellow chubby cat, Charlie, normally reticent to being held, jumped in Sylvie's lap and purred. At last, Sylvie started breathing again.

"They give me three months tops. Damn it! I'm only sixty-three years old." Sylvie pounded the arm of her chair with her fist, scaring Charlie off her lap. "How do I even start this *dying*?"

Wade leaned in and squeezed her hand. "What do you mean 'start dying'? Though my heart is breaking to even have this conversation, sweetheart, it seems to me that it's the perfect time to start living. Let's focus on that."

And so she did.

Within days, her children arrived—Matt, his wife Ellen, and the kids. Then Kelsey and her fiancé, Jason. Even Christopher, normally devoted to his architecture firm, dropped his West Coast meeting to come. They didn't know what to say but tiptoed around the house with heads tilted as they watched her. Sylvie refused to accept their pity. She donned hiking boots and asked, "Who's joining me?"

"It's raining," they said in chorus.

"So, let's hike in the rain. I'm leaving in fifteen."

The trail behind her house always soothed her. She had talks with her children as teens on this path. Something about being side-by-side—not face-to-face—made the conversations easier. The morning drizzle covered them.

Christopher slowed his pace to be next to her. "This blows Mom. I guess our New Year's Eve list has taken on a different meaning now."

Since Christopher was thirteen, he and Sylvie made goals for the year instead of resolutions. They called it their "Try-Something-New List." But it was more than that. It was intention for a life carefully lived. Christopher was like that, constantly evaluating. He lived his life so purely.

"I don't remember putting cancer on the list," Sylvie pointed out.

Christopher took her hand as they walked. "Not at all. But you mentioned taking a trip with your sisters. Why don't you do it?"

"We're likely to kill each other if we're in the same room."

"So...what do you have to lose, then?"

Sylvie laughed. "Good point. Besides, they have to be nice to me if I tell them I'm dying."

Matt's oldest squealed with delight as Wade swung her in the air, the echoes of joy reverberating over Sylvie's head. In hushed tones, Kelsey and Jason huddled up with Ellen. Sylvie suspected they discussed their wedding plans, scheduled for early next year. "Without Mom," she heard. "Deposit back" shortly after. She slowed to walk with them, and silence followed. Matt hung behind as if he'd catch her if she keeled over. When the downpour arrived, they all darted for the house. The next morning, Sylvie convinced them all to go home after promising one last family trip to the mountains early next month.

Their neighbors and friends heard the news, either from Wade or the neighborhood newsletter prayer list, and showed up in force with casseroles the first week: chicken enchiladas, tuna noodle, and eight different versions of macaroni and cheese. Their closest neighbor, Monica, offered to manage the food brigade for them. Sylvie suggested two meals per week, then added, "Find a good home for all these mac-and-cheese casseroles. Our freezer is full. You mentioned your friend took in her teen grandson. Give her one."

In the days that followed, she and Wade drove to Indianapolis for a second opinion. Sylvie tripped and fell in the clinic, prompting a flurry of doctor examinations beyond those already scheduled. At the end of the day, everyone agreed with the first diagnosis. Her nervous system had already begun its decline. They suggested she walk with a cane to help with balance issues. Wade cried as they drove away.

"Pull over," Sylvie said. "I'll drive home since my eyes are dry." *This might be my last time behind the wheel.*

When Wade's tears didn't stop, she pulled into a roadside rest stop and held him while the car ran.

Wade removed his glasses, wiped his eyes, and held her face close to his. "I don't want to live my life without you, Hun. What we have is perfect."

"You can, and you will." Sylvie's heart pounded. She exhaled to calm herself before she continued. "I'll say this now, and I want you to hear me. Allow yourself to love when I'm gone. Do you remember our estate attorney saying that a line of women would beat down your door with casseroles if I died first?" Her voice broke, but she forced the words out with a pitch an octave higher. "So here we are. Give it time—a year to show your love for me *and* to avoid gossip. Then be ready to go on." She pulled herself back and placed her hands in his to quell the shaking, and exhaled. "But I'm counting on you to keep my memory alive, babe. Talk to the kids about me. The grandkids, too. I'll be watching with joy and waiting for you. My dear, thank you for this life."

They stayed at the roadside rest stop until twilight came. No words. Just presence. Wade drove them home as they held hands.

When Wade left for his next business trip—the last one this quarter—Sylvie walked him to the car. As he drove out of view, she watched him until he turned the corner and disappeared from sight. Sylvie sat down in the grass to avoid being in her house alone. She grabbed a tall milkweed that sprouted out of place and pulled it apart to let it return to the earth. She lay back and peered through the leaves of the large elm out front. They had started to turn and danced in front of her—beckoning. Finally, she pulled herself up before any of the neighbors saw her and reported her behavior to Wade. She returned to the house to watch home movies of their children, then recorded videos of her own for them after she passed. One for Kelsey's wedding, if she wasn't there. One for Christopher about her ultimate try-something-new experience. Oh, how her heart broke to speak aloud to them. She heated leftover chicken soup from the Care Calendar delivery while she waited for red eyes to clear up. Then she finished recording the rest of the messages. She would miss her family so much. But would she? Is that how death worked?

With her doctor's permission after her first seizure and overnight hospital stay, they drove to their mountain cabin after Wade's return, arriving a day early to make the beds and stock the fridge before their kids arrived. Wade did the lion's share of the work as Sylvie nursed the pain in her head. She had narcotics if needed, but kept them at bay to be coherent for the last gathering of her family. As she looked out the front window, a green van pulled up, and a man brought two bouquets and one floral arrangement toward their front door.

"Wa-ade," Sylvie called. "Can you stop that delivery man from bringing all those flowers to the wrong house?"

Wade opened the front door enough to allow the man entry. "Put them on the dining room table."

"What's going on?"

"I want Kelsey to tell you. Can you stay curious until she and Jason arrive?"

"Those look like wedding flowers."

"Honey, those *are* wedding flowers. Don't make me say anything more."

Before long, Kelsey and Jason pulled up and unloaded their suitcases from the trunk of their car. Jason carried a long white travel bag. Without words, Sylvie knew they had sacrificed their dream wedding to have a simple one she could attend. They were getting married this weekend. She stood to greet them and held herself against the wingback chair for balance. "What's going on?"

Kelsey hiccupped the words. "I couldn't imagine my wedding without you, Mom. I didn't tell you because you'd try to talk me out of it."

Before she could scold them, the rest of the family arrived, and chaos unfolded. The next morning, a hairdresser showed up to do Kelsey's hair and makeup. Jason's parents and his younger brother, who served as their photographer, joined them after a four-hour drive. Sylvie walked Kelsey down the aisle, then joined Wade on the sofa near the fireplace. Ellen, with elegance and grace, performed the ceremony. Sylvie held it together until Ellen announced the words "Till death do you part." Sylvie gasped and leaned her head on Wade's shoulder, sucking in her grief until the ceremony was over. To the beat of Kelsey and Jason's recessional song, a parade of memories of her daughter flashed through Sylvie's mind—Kelsey twirling in her favorite dress at the age of five, falling asleep on Wade's shoulder after hikes, and cuddling with her stuffed bunny when she had the flu. Kelsey and Jason stopped in front of her and eased Sylvie off the sofa. They wrapped their arms around her as they swayed to the music. Time slowed down. Sylvie couldn't hold back the happy tears.

Rather than a honeymoon, Kelsey and Jason stayed at the house for four days of family antics of every kind: game night, bonfires, snipe hunts with Matt's kids, and a walk to Sunset Point, where they all hugged and cried. It would be her last time here. On their walk back to the cabin, someone sang *We Are Family*. Christopher could see her struggle to walk on the uneven ground, and attempted to carry her on his back. Sylvie laughed so hard that Christopher fell in a pile of autumn leaves, and dumped her, which started a leaf fight. They all said their goodbyes a few days later, promising another family weekend soon.

When Sylvie and Wade arrived home, Monica waved from next door and came across the side lawn. "If you aren't too tired, Sylvie, will you join me on my back porch for a drink and snacks for a bit? We both know Wade will unload the car."

"Go on," Wade said. "I got this."

Sylvie stumbled in the grass, and Monica took her arm to help her negotiate the lawn to her house. Monica helped Sylvie recline in the patio chair and covered her with a light blanket. "It's getting chilly already. Relax while I get some wine. You can still drink, right?"

"As long as I haven't taken pain meds. Anyway, what harm could it do now?"

Monica returned with chocolates and cheese with crackers—Sylvie's two favorite food groups. Monica sat across from her in silence until Sylvie raised a glass. "Cheers. To many more."

"We both know that's not true, Sylvie. You don't have to pretend with me." Monica patted Sylvie's outstretched legs.

Sylvie weakly smiled. "Can I ask you something? I know you're a church-going Catholic. Am I a bad person if I'm not sure there's something after this—a heaven? I don't know. Maybe my spirit will float around or become part of something bigger than me. I have threatened to haunt Wade if he sulks more than a year."

Sylvie laughed, backing away from the serious conversation.

Monica took her hand. "You couldn't be a bad person if you tried, sweet friend. I believe your spirit will live on in those you've loved, as some sort of a connection to others. A form of perfect love that will never go away."

"I like that. Thank you. Sorry to weigh you down."

"You didn't. I love you, you know that. You can say anything to me. But...if we have the serious topics taken care of, I'd like to ask about a practical matter. Here, have some truffles. Good for the soul."

Sylvie popped one into her mouth. "What practical matter?"

"Well, more casseroles are coming in than we asked. We have about five aluminum tins right now too many. My freezer is full. What would you like me to do with them?"

"I hate to shut the food train down. It's how people are showing that they care. I mean, what else can they do when they hear our awful news? How about this? Wade can take some to the women's shelter where I volunteered. I bet they'd love some mac and cheese."

"They would. It's a shame that more people can't benefit from this outpouring." Monica pulled her long dark hair up into a ponytail. "Hmmm. I have an idea. Could I use your meal train for a greater cause?"

"What do you mean?"

"Can I change the name of your online calendar to something like *Mac and Cheese Love?* Then open it up for daily casserole deliveries—to be given to people who would benefit from knowing that someone cares. If anyone knows of a person in need, they could request one for them. I get their name and contact info and match them with a donation casserole and a time for them to deliver it. I'll be the clearinghouse. What do you think?"

"I love the idea. Instead of kindness coming to me, it goes through me." Sylvie laughed. "Whoa, the wine is making me loopy. Are you sure you have the time and energy for this?"

"Are you kidding? Thomas is in high school. As long as I pay for gas in his car, he's happy. In fact, he could help deliver. It'd be my pleasure to do this in your name."

Her sisters came into town for a weekend, and Wade offered to find a hotel room so the women could have the house. He stocked it with some casseroles, plenty of wine and coffee, and told her he was a phone call away if she needed him. "We'll be all right."

"You sound so sure. You haven't forgotten the last family reunion, right? Cindy slapping your hand because you cut the onions too small. You almost punched her."

Sylvie bit her lower lip at the reminder. "No one will get hurt," she promised, although she wasn't exactly sure about that considering their history.

The long-held resentments between them broke during a card game.

Cindy, the oldest, advised Sylvie about the best way to die. "Don't make your family go through the agony, Sylvie. There are hospice facilities, you know."

"Excuse me?" Sylvie turned to face Cindy.

Jenny, the youngest, flipped up the card table and screamed, "Cindy, just stop it, will you?"

Then Sylvie started laughing and smeared a two-finger scoop of the macaroni and cheese casserole on Cindy's face, prompting them all to get involved, slinging food at each other. When Cindy held Sylvie with one arm to attack with a gooey mess of yellow congealed cheese, Sylvie reversed her hold and hugged her. They went from laughter to crying, their tears intermingling with globs of food.

Jenny found them kitchen towels to clean up themselves and the mess. "Remember how Mom always used to say that we went together like peanut butter and jelly? She'd mix it up and say 'peaches and cream' sometimes. She never mentioned macaroni and cheese, did she?"

That night, Sylvie and Jenny stayed up to reminisce. When Sylvie stood to go to the bathroom, a searing pain pierced the base of her skull. It tingled on her left side, and a streak of wavy darkness filled her vision. Sylvie grabbed Jenny and screamed. "Get help!"

Jenny called 911 and Wade, woke Cindy, and followed the ambulance to the emergency room. When Wade came into Sylvie's room and pushed her hair out of her face, she slurred, "I'm hurt, honey. I'm sorry I broke my promise."

The next weeks passed quickly, with medical assessments, lawyer visits, and a not-her-best-day trip to the funeral home. Sylvie became upset when Wade insisted on a plot—a place for him to visit. *A hole in the ground.* Why should it matter? She'd be dead, anyway. But being in the ground eternally disturbed her. After pounding her cane on the wooden floor, Sylvie left in a huff—right foot leading, left foot dragging—to go to the car. Over coffee that afternoon, Wade apologized and conceded that cremation or burial was her decision. They should do whatever she wanted. As a peace offering, he suggested what he called a *Big Ass Party* before her death instead of a celebration of life after. She loved the idea. The next day, she listed the names of everyone important to her for the invitations—childhood friends, her high school boyfriend and his wife, her favorite boss, neighbors, soccer friends, and family—and asked Wade's sister to help him plan it while she napped.

With permission from Sylvie's doctor, their three best couple friends joined Sylvie and Wade on a spa retreat at a nearby resort. Donna hired a shaman to perform a blessing ritual, complete with burning sage, to "purify and sanctify" the bond between them. During the ceremony, Sylvie broke down, and as her friends gathered to comfort her, circling her with hugs and support, they soon realized that she had been consumed by one of her laughing fits, revealed by her signature snort. Nina ushered her out of the room, saying, "There, there, now," as she patted Sylvie's arm, going along with the ruse of distress to avoid insulting the shaman.

Poor Nina—she would be lost when Sylvie died. Their weekly lunch date after Nina's son's suicide last year kept her going. She'd ask Monica to deliver food to Nina for a while, just to make sure she had weekly contact in Sylvie's place.

The day of the party arrived. A large tent had been set up in the backyard with heaters to ward off the promised cold front. Wade spared no expense, hiring Sylvie's favorite food truck to feed the crowd. An open bar was set up in a corner with the best champagne to toast Sylvie. A male guitarist played acoustic music from their teen years. Monica had offered to put up a photo booth with silly props for friends to take their last photo with her. Sylvie engaged Ellen to be her right-hand woman, to assist her as needed since she couldn't lift herself from a chair any longer. Sylvie looked around. All of her favorite people were here, and *she was alive to see them*. Across the way, Sylvie caught eyes with her first love, Peter. He came over and hugged her awkwardly as she sat on her stool. "Still as beautiful as ever, Syl. You sure know how to break a man's heart. You always have. I'm happy to see you so happy. What a life well lived." It mattered to Sylvie to hear these words. She would take them to her grave—if only she had agreed to one.

Matt's kids, Chase and Julia, hung back, not sure how to talk about her dying. Finally, eight-year-old Chase came forward, pulling his little sister Julia with him. He thrust a card at her, with a hand-drawn angel on the envelope. "Mommy says this will make you feel better. But it's just a card I made."

With Ellen's help, Sylvie moved to a table with chairs around it, so she could sit at the children's level. "Let me open this card right now." They smiled at each other when she exclaimed, "A firefly! How did you know that I love fireflies?"

Chase puckered his lower lip. "We didn't know. But Grammy, we don't want you to die. We don't want you to be dead forever."

Sylvie hugged him and used her thumbs to wipe his tears. "Listen, I have something very important to tell you."

Julia took her hand and leaned in.

"I'm going to visit you sometimes from heaven. But I won't look like I do now. I'll be a firefly that visits when it starts to get dark. So, whenever you see one flying around, think of me. Is that our deal? I'll love you forever."

They nodded, hanging onto her until Ellen untangled them and escorted them back to Sylvie and Wade's home to put them to bed.

Other treasured conversations happened, words that lifted her higher than any heaven could. To her surprise, there were more laughs than tears. That night, she lay in Wade's arms and just smiled, fighting sleep to have this day last forever. "You did it, babe. It was the best Big Ass Party I've ever attended."

"That's because it was your Big Ass Party. You better get some sleep. By the way, you have an interview tomorrow." His voice was gruff after drinking whiskey and talking with friends all evening.

"What are you talking about? With Saint Peter?" She teased with her morbid joke.

He laughed. "Not with God. Not tomorrow, anyway. The Sunday Lifestyle reporter contacted Monica. They want to interview you about *Mac and Cheese Love*. They're doing a big feature about the nonprofit Monica created in your name."

Wade yawned and drifted off. Sylvie stayed awake, remembering each conversation of the night. Her children's banter, cementing a friendship that would get them through after she was gone. Antidotes about past adventures with friends, which would be retold after she passed. Planting images of fireflies to keep her memory alive. The camaraderie of her sisters as they continued their bond without her. The love had filled the backyard tent and her dying heart. Enough love to lift her all the way to high heaven. Enough love to carry Wade after she passed. Enough to comfort those who needed it in their community after she was gone. All of it just as gooey as a casserole of macaroni and cheese.

About Kimberly Nixon

Kimberly Nixon writes family-driven stories featuring strong, determined—sometimes wild—characters inspired by real people. She wrangles these vivid personalities into the heart of her fiction, crafting emotionally rich narratives rooted in resilience and grit. Her novels *Rock Bottom, Tennessee* and *Rock Bottom Rising* are based on the true story of her grandmother's felony conviction in 1925 Appalachia. Kimberly is also the author of the forthcoming children's book *A Visit with Grandypants*, set to release this fall. A member of the Women's Fiction Writers Association and the Writers' League of Texas, she lives in Austin, Texas with her husband Paul and is committed to living a great story of her own.

For more information about Kimberly and updates, go to: https://kimberlynixon.com/

Acknowledgements

This anthology would not have been possible without the generosity, feedback, and creativity of all the contributors who supported this idea by submitting their stories. Your words brought the theme of kindness to life in ways that are moving, heartfelt, and inspiring.

Special thanks to Amanda Speights and Heidi, McIntyre whose thoughtful input helped us decide on the perfect cover. To Paulette Stout, for carefully formatting the manuscripts and making sure every story found its place. And to Erica Haraldsen, The Story Keeper Book Coach, for providing extra support during the beta reading process and helping shape the final collection.

Most of all, thank you to every reader who picks up this book. May these stories remind you of the power of kindness in our everyday lives.

Janet Koops

www.ingramcontent.com/pod-product-compliance
Lightning Source LLC
Chambersburg PA
CBHW020323260626
47156CB00004B/1344